THE OUIJA BOARD SAID IT WAS HUNGRY

BRANDON WILLS

I dedicate this book to my friend Henry, who sadly took his life at the young age of 19 in 2009. I hope he will be proud of me and how far I've come. I miss you, Henry.

CONTENTS

FOREWORD

Warning: some of these stories include triggering things like suicide, murder, rape, and sexual assault.

Some of these stories were painful to revisit. They were written during difficult times of my life. I've often found that writing is therapeutic and would often help to heal from these chaotic eras. I am glad my life is no longer this way and my writing has drastically improved. These stories have all been edited before I published them in this book, so they are not exactly the originals. I hope you will enjoy this collection and spread the word about me and my writings!

Brandon Wills

THE OUIJA BOARD SAID IT WAS HUNGRY

MY NAME IS HENRY HIMURA. I work for a large law firm situated near downtown Los Angeles. We've overseen some of the biggest, most controversial cases in the last two decades and have built quite a name for ourselves. I am using a pseudonym because, as you will hear, this story is almost fantastical, too frightening to believe real. I don't want to ruin a career I have spent so much time and effort building just because some people don't want to believe the truth of what's out there. First, I want to issue a warning: never, ever play kokkuri-san. No matter how innocent the internet or books may make it sound, please don't do it. This is the story of how my life changed forever and how I lost something so dear.

Spirit boards come in all shapes and sizes and various names as well. In the U.S., the most common one is an Ouija board. They are intended as children's games when, really, you can unleash something so powerful and evil that it may never be bottled. Spirit boards are just a portal to the other side, a way for spirits to communicate directly with the living, and that spirit can be a good or a total evil menace. According to my research, you can use almost anything as your spirit board.

In my native country of Japan, we played a game called kokkuri-san. With this game, you question the spirits about your future, and they will sometimes answer, maybe not with the answer you seek. We would take a coin, place it on paper with some words and numbers written on it, and the coin would slide across to answer your question. After you were finished, you were supposed to tell Kokkuri-san to go home, slide the coin to the red torii symbol at the top of the paper, and then tear the paper into forty-eight pieces or burn it.

Almost thirty years ago, my siblings and I started playing kokkuri-san a dozen or so times before moving to America without much more than a few funny responses from the fox spirit. The last time we played kokkuri-san, my brother asked the spirit, "Kokkuri-san, kokkuri-san, will you move this coin?"

The coin slid across the paper in repeated circles for a few seconds, then stopped.

"Kokkuri-san, when will I become rich and famous?" he asked.

The coin slid slowly across the paper, pressing so hard against the paper that I thought it would tear, but we were barely pressing on it—something else was doing it. It spelled out:

F E E D

Then, a pause.

M E

From behind us, somewhere in the dark, came a deep guttural growl, like that of a hungry dog; we didn't own a dog. We knew this was not kokkuri-san. It was never described to act like this or to be threatening; something else had come through the game! My brother panicked, running across the room to grab Father's lighter from his desk drawer. He set the paper on fire, dropped it into the sink to burn, and then turned on the tap to drown out the flames. I realize his mistake now, something that I wish he would've done, and maybe it could've prevented everything that would come. He forgot to tell the kokkuri-san to go home before destroying the paper; he left it trapped in our world.

A few weeks later, our father transferred his job with a car manufacturer to the U.S., and we moved to Seattle. At first, adjusting to the culture shock was overwhelming, but we had all taken English language classes in school, which made it easier. I can remember a day that we went into a toy store, and we were shocked to see that there was a popular, widely sold board game that was like kokkuri-san, the Ouija board. Our mother forbade us from buying it, saying it would only invite trouble, and she was unaware that we had already played kokkuri-san numerous times by then.

My brother and I managed to sneak over to the store and bought the Ouija board later that week. Katsuro was the most eager to buy it, which was obvious. I asked him why.

"Every night since the last time we played kokkuri-san, I've had these nightmares. They're too real—sometimes, I think they happen to me. In those dreams, I'm lying in bed, and from the corner of my eye, I can see a dark shadow beside me. I can hear it taking deep, gasping breaths and dripping saliva like it is starving. It speaks to me in a growl, demanding that I feed it."

I asked him, "Did you ask what it wants?"

Deep in thought, he paused momentarily as we walked down the sidewalk back home. "No, I always wake up, and I can't move for a long time. Sometimes, I swear it is standing beside the bed, waiting for me to feed it... or feed on me." I could see the fear in his eyes and his voice. I had no doubt he was telling the truth.

"Maybe you are just dreaming, Katsuro. Dreams sometimes seem real, but they're not; they're—."

"Dreams don't breathe into your ear while you're lying on your back and unable to scream, or yell, or do anything!"

I could only hang my head in shame because I felt terrible for doubting my brother. I wanted to believe him, but who could believe something so outrageous without seeing it yourself?

Katsuro was never one to lie and would practically break his neck to tell the truth. "Okay, what do you want to do with the Ouija board?"

"I want to speak to it, banish it back to hell, then burn that board. We'll play by the rules this time, and it won't follow us!" He was dead serious and had the bravery of someone far older than twelve. Tears were streaming down his cheeks as he clenched his fists, his stride becoming faster and faster. That happened on a Monday.

Our parents would be out the following Friday to a dinner with some of father's executives to welcome him to the USA, and they said they would be out for hours. I was in charge because I was the oldest at fifteen, so I had to keep an eye on my siblings. Michiko was fourteen at the time and was too preoccupied with the wonderment of American television, so Katsuro and I decided to leave her out of the plan, and we also felt like it was a favor to our only sister to leave her out of any chaos that might happen.

I could read English well, but my siblings weren't so great. Of course, the Ouija board was in English, so I would have to translate because Katsuro couldn't. We unboxed the 'game,' reading the rules aloud.

'Never play alone.' Check.

'Never play in a graveyard.' Check. It made me double-think if any were nearby, but I didn't believe there were.

'Never burn it.' This one Katsuro became frustrated over. "Why not?!" he cried, bemoaning.

"I don't know, Katsuro. It doesn't say. They're just the rules, and I don't think questioning them would be a good idea."

Never leave the planchette on the board. "Why not?" he asked.

"I don't know. I suppose it would leave the doorway open? Stop questioning the rules and listen!"

"Okay! Fine!"

'Never ask when you will die.'

And the last rule: 'Don't forget to say goodbye.' "That's the one we forgot with kokkuri-san!" Katsuro reminded me.

Thunder was rolling outside, and it sounded remarkably close to the house. Then lightning crashed, casting the whole house in a bright light like a camera flash.

"Yes, Katsuro, and let's not do that again." I put the rules back into the box and slammed my palms on the table. "If you try to break any of these rules, I will not be to blame if something gets you!"

"I won't!"

"Good. Now, let's hurry before—"

That was when the lights went off. Katsuro flipped the light switch several times with no effect. I remember groaning with indignation at the annoyance. What I hadn't noticed then, and I wish I would have, was that Michiko never asked what happened or even made a sound about the power going out. You will see why later.

"No! It shut off the lights! It's onto our plan!" The fear was growing in his voice.

"Shut up, Katsuro! It's probably the storm! Get those candles that Mother keeps for emergencies! Hurry!"

Katsuro fetched the candles with an eagerness I rarely saw in him. He was at a running pace, and I couldn't see him, but I heard him rummaging through cabinets frantically, followed by the patting of his feet coming back down the hallway.

"Got 'em!"

"Okay. I hope you didn't break anything," I said as I leered at him. "Anyway, let's light them around the table so we can see the board better."

"I wish the power were working," his voice was quaking. "I do, too, but we'll have to wait for the power company to fix it."

I struck a match, but it went out with an abrupt hiss. I thought the match was just a dud, so I struck another, and the same thing happened. My annoyance was building at this point. I struck another and another; they snuffed out within a second of being lit. My brother found a stick lighter and tried that, but it did the same thing. No gust or blowing of the air conditioner could have caused that since the power was out. Finally, after several attempts, the spirit allowed us to light our candles as if mocking us.

We began to play kokkuri-san on the Ouija board. Katsuro went to the window by the dining room table and opened it. The ozone smell of the thunderstorm flooded the inside of the house, and the loud rumbling of thunder filled the house. We removed the planchette from the box and placed it at the bottom. After a few moments of hesitation, we touched the planchette and started the game.

"Kokkuri-san, Kokkuri-san, if you're here, please move this… planchette," my brother said, unsure if he was saying the word correctly. He pronounced it more like 'blanket,' but I just shrugged and laughed. In case you haven't seen an Ouija board, the planchette is the triangular piece that players put their hands on and is used by the spirits to point to letters and numbers.

Within an instant, it began spelling out:

H U N G R Y

"What does it say, Henry?"

"It says it is hungry," I replied, almost crying in fear. I was unsure why I was afraid, but something about how it jumped straight to its demand was blood-chilling. "Did you move it? Did you?"

"No! I would never do that, Henry! I didn't!" I believed him and could feel the tightening grip of fear in my stomach.

To the point, Katsuro asked, "What do you want to eat?"

The planchette moved with such force that I remember having trouble keeping my fingers on it, letting go to see if it'd move on its own.

M E A T

I nearly flung my hands off the planchette and ran out of the room, but I reminded myself that I was the older one and I had to be strong for my little brother. I also wasn't sure what'd happen to us if I did let go.

"I will find you something," Katsuro answered, nearly jumping from his chair. He was dashing toward the fridge.

"No! Please do not give it what it wants! You'll make it—," that was all I got out before a sheering pain went down my back, a pain so intense that I found it hard to breathe. I fell to the floor, writhing in the sudden, screaming pain. Gasping, I moved my hand under my shirt. I winced as it touched the pained area and saw blood when I looked at it.

"Katsuro! Look at my back! Please!" He dug through the refrigerator by then, almost ignoring me, looking desperately for something to offer.

He casually looked over his shoulder, "I'll be right there!" he said as he shut the fridge and came running over to me, his little arms carrying wrapped ground beef that he sat on the table. He looked at my back and gasped.

"Henry! Three long scratches are going all the way down your back! What happened!?"

"It was that spirit! It did that when I told you not to feed it! You're just going to make it stronger, Katsuro!"

We made eye contact with the ground beef, but the packages were empty. There was no sign that the packaging had been cut, torn, or broken into—just empty packages. The planchette moved again, this time without us touching it. It moved with a jerky motion, like something didn't quite know what it was doing, like the jerky movement of computer lag.

NEXT

The planchette slid to a blank area and back onto the board.

BLOOD

Katsuro grabbed the planchette and threw it out the window as hard as his little arms could. When we turned around, it was on the table with the word NO.

It began to spell out.

YOURS

I moved the planchette to the word NO and then to GOOD-BYE, but then it moved on its own back to the word NO and spelled the next word so fast that I could barely tell that it said:

SISTER

Michiko gave out a terrifying scream so loud that somebody would've called the police if they could've heard her over the storm. Katsuro and I rushed down the hallway to her room at the far right of the hallway. She was lying on her side under the blankets, facing the wall, still screaming. I rolled her over to examine her; her eyes were shut as if she were in a deep sleep, but her mouth was shrieking in bloody terror.

I shook her hard several times, calling her name and trying my best to wake her, but she just kept screaming. Her arm flopped from under the blanket over the side of the bed as I was shaking her, and I saw that her wrist was slowly dripping blood onto the carpet. It wasn't slit on the artery or anything life—threatening, but pricked, like with a small knife, and was only bleeding a few drops at a time. I knew First Aid, so I wrapped the wound with one of her clean socks from her dresser and told Katsuro we had to end this now.

As we were leaving Michiko's room, the temperature in the house plummeted, which was unexplainable since it was late summer. The air conditioning wasn't working due to the power outage. I noticed that my breath was coming out in a cloud. The lights began to flicker then, and I saw something standing at the end of the hallway: a pitch-black figure about seven feet tall, nearly as high as the ceiling! It looked like a man but had long, skinny claws instead of hands and a smile filled with pointed teeth. It was gone once the flickering stopped a few moments later. It showed us what it was, and I knew it was warning us to continue… or else.

Katsuro and I sat at the table and placed our hands on the board.

"What can we do to make you go away?"

The planchette moved to NO, then GOODBYE.

My brother sighed but then gave out a shriek of terror as he was jerked to the floor and dragged down the hallway by some invisible force. I jumped up, grabbing his hands, pulling with everything I had, but I couldn't budge him. It was going straight into his closet. He kept screaming, "No! Please, no! Stop! Just stop!" as he was being forced down the hallway and inside his bedroom closet. From within the closet, I saw yellow eyes and a broad smile staring back at me. I grabbed Katsuro's hands, trying my best to stop it, but it was useless; the closet snapped shut with a hard and powerful slam, and Katsuro went inside.

Out of panic and desperation, I tried to open the closet doors. After multiple attempts, the doors finally opened. My brother was not inside. Inside were piles of Styrofoam meat trays—all appeared to have been opened recently. I realized later that Katsuro had been spending his allowance on various kinds of meats for this thing. I also found another kokkuri-san paper under some of the trays. I tore it into forty-eight pieces, along with the Ouija board, burned them, and threw the ashes into the wind, thinking it might summon him back. It didn't.

He did not.

It has been nearly twenty years since he went missing, and we filed that missing person report. My parents assumed that he ran away to go back to Japan. The move had been hard on him, and he expressed his dislike of the move often. As for the meat trays, my parents and the police didn't mention that detail or ask about it if they didn't notice them. I searched for my brother for weeks, finding no trace of him. Sometimes, I'd sit in his closet, begging for an answer, but I'd get nothing. My parents grieved for a long time, and their marriage dissolved as a result. Mother returned to Japan, while she allowed father to keep us in America, where I finished school and later became a lawyer. My father once convinced me to pay a private investigator to find Katsuro, but as you may guess, they found no trace of him either.

After I wrote this, an Ouija board was on my dining room table. On the table, I also have some cheap ground beef, my brother's favorite toy, and something I didn't have thirty years ago: a vast knowledge of how to kill a demon.

LEAVING IT ALL BEHIND

THE RATCHET CRANKED in his busted hand. The knuckles on his right hand were caked in dried blood and grease. Kor's hand ached and was stiffened into the shape that holds the ratchet. He had been tightening bolts for hours, attaching the outer shell to the rocket. He had painted the entire shell in blaze orange with a bright red lightning bolt down both sides, outlined in black. He had christened it "The Bolt."

"Kor! Come eat your damn dinner already!" his wife yelled out the back door.

He decided now was the time to quit for the day before her anger simmered to an explosive boil. The chilly nighttime air blew in through the barn's open doors, but it did little to cool his over-worked body. Finally, the last bolt was tightened. Kor wiped his hands with an old rag as he stood back to admire his life's work. He had found this old Ingoldt Model TR-3B in a scrap yard twenty years ago. Twenty years before that, it had most likely been the toy of a rich kid who used it to zoom to the moon and back to show off with his girlfriend. At forty years old, Kor was satisfied that it was ready for a test flight, but he wouldn't tell his wife.

Stiff-legged and exhausted, Kor shuffled inside, hastily ate his dinner, showered, and collapsed into bed. All night, he dreamed of the burning excitement he had longed for. He had completed the safety checks and climbed into the cockpit. He flipped the switch to activate the power, then the switch to prime the thruster. As it heated up, he started the engine and heard it roar to life. The loud winding of the jet engine was growing as if the rocket were dying for its first flight in those long forty years.

"Kor! Wake the hell up! All you want to do is sleep anymore! The cows need to be fed, the chicken eggs need to be collected, and the horses need to be brushed! I need you to do all this before you start tinkering with that… toy!"

So close.

His wife had interrupted yet another glorious dream of escaping from his never-ending hell. When he bought the rocket twenty years ago, he still loved his wife dearly. She was happy, beautiful, and still as vibrant as the sun. Now, she was nearly always angry with him, her beauty had faded into a constant grimace, and she was always finding a way to boss him around—all those things had completely removed any feelings of affection he had for her.

Kor grabbed a clean pair of overalls and headed toward the backdoor to start his chores.

"Now, listen, Kor. I'm going to my mother's for the weekend. I might even stay a week. I don't know yet. I need to get away from this place for a while."

"Me too," he thought.

"Okay, dear," he replied instead, turning around and trudging toward the animals.

He was in the middle of collecting the chicken eggs when it dawned on him.

"Now's my chance."

There were nice places on the moon in those days. It had been fifty years since the first city had been founded. It was completely enclosed in a dome, fed by massive oxygen tanks that were refilled weekly from shipments that came from Earth. Now there are ten more cities. Kor was always seeing jobs listed in ads saying that there were some nice retirement communities up there with a great view of the Earth. Hell, he had even seen factory jobs offering a complimentary apartment on company property. Anything would be better than being stuck in a life with a wife who didn't love him anymore.

Kor toiled for a few hours, but he finished the chores. He dashed inside the house. In his closet, he found an old suitcase that hadn't been used since their first vacation to Bermuda thirty-six years before. The dust was so thick that it had to be wiped off with his sleeve. Inside, he found an old picture of them on that trip—a young, happy, content, and able-bodied couple embracing each other with grins as wide as their faces.

"Time isn't fair," he thought.

He sat the photo on the bed and packed a week's worth of clothes. About a year ago, he had driven down to the courthouse to get the documents necessary to file for divorce. Kor tried to work up the nerve, but he was so afraid of his wife that he could never work it up to do it. He had already signed his part—the ink had long dried, along with a few fresh tears, and he left the rest on the bed for her to complete, he retrieved the ladder he was going to use to climb into the cockpit and the suit he had bought from the junkyard that was in near-mint.

Outside, Kor climbed onto his tractor to pull the rocket out of the barn toward a concrete pad that he'd placed in the middle of his field, just for this purpose, a long time ago. In the barn, he retrieved the ladder he was going to use to climb into the cockpit and the suit he had bought from the junkyard that was in near mint condition.

Kor evaluated the oxygen tanks and ensured he could breathe in the suit. He also checked that the suit had no holes. At the rocket, he ran over a safety checklist on a clipboard, flying through it with the gleeful excitement a child might have on their way to a theme park. Check, check, and more checks. He could barely contain his excitement.

Kor dashed up the ladder, nearly tripping twice on the way up. He had spent a long time fixing the cockpit. It took him over a decade to collect all the necessary parts from scrappers and dealers online. After all his efforts, it looked brand spanking new. He had spent the last week polishing and refining all the buttons, screens, and coverings. He had also rigorously assessed each dial, sensor, and knob. The rocket radiated with the infamous new car smell. His grin stretched from ear to ear.

The seat belt snapped with a crisp click; the straps tightened perfectly. He flipped the switch to turn on the power and the switch to prime the thruster. The engine roared to life. It was even better than in his dream. The vibrations made the floor hum with life. From his position, he could see the approaching evening sky. The moon had already appeared as if greeting him. While tending to the animals, he had looked up the evening's best time to launch for his area. It would arrive in three minutes.

He dug through his bag to double-check that he had brought all the necessary documents to immigrate to the moon and found that he had accidentally packed the picture of him and his wife from all those years ago in Bermuda. He unbuckled from his seat, staring at it for several moments, remembering their good times.

No, he thought, this was my old life. He tossed the old photo out the door. It fluttered down to the ground, landing below the thrusters on the launchpad.

"This is Delta 24-28-39. Am I clear to launch?" Kor said into his radio to the FAA.

"Roger that. You are clear for takeoff," the attendant replied. "Roger. Launching in T-Minus 30 seconds."

"Roger that, Delta 24-38-39."

He flipped the switch to ignite the flames of the thruster, which would build up the pressure needed to launch.

"T-minus ten!" He yelled as he set coordinates in his guidance system.

"Zero!"

He flipped the final switch. The thrusters roared to life. Kor was yanked back in his seat with such force that it slammed his teeth together in a painful wave. Soon, he was almost out of the troposphere. The rocket jerked as he entered the stratosphere, then the mesosphere.

About halfway through the mesosphere, the rocket began to rattle violently, so much so that he could barely keep his hands on the controls. Nothing Kor had read said that was normal. He began to panic. He debated whether he should abandon the flight and turn it around immediately... but was so close. It was just one more layer before he was free. Could he last just a few more agonizing minutes?

Kor decided to persevere. This old relic was tough. He spent so much time on it that it was basically brand new again. The cockpit began to get extremely hot, baking him like a sauna.

Sweat poured down his face into his eyes. At first, he thought it was just his nerves, but then he realized his soles were also starting to get hot.

Something was going very wrong.

Flames erupted from the engine compartment into the cockpit from underneath. His seat began to melt underneath him. The nearly mint condition suit began to melt into his skin. The pain was unbearably excruciating. He cried out in agony as he frantically tried to reach for the ejection button, but he realized that the shaking rocket and the g-forces made it impossible for him to reach it.

For some reason, at that moment, all he could think of was his wife. He thought of them in their younger days, of that trip to

Bermuda, of the ocean waves lapping over his feet as they sipped fruity drinks at that nice resort. The sun warmed and tanned his young skin. The love they made in the hotel every night as the moon shone through the open blinds. He almost wanted to smile.

The explosion killed him instantly.

I PLAYED THE BLAIR WITCH GAME AND SHE'S STALKING ME

BEFORE I BEGIN, I GUESS I'll tell you about myself, which may establish some credibility. My name is Mason, and I am a 35-year-old third-grade English teacher in a suburb outside of Columbus, Ohio. As far as I know, I've never had a history of hallucinating, physically or audibly. I've been married once and divorced, and I have no kids. My husky, Dagger, is probably the closest I'll ever come to having a kid. Now that you know all that, I hope you can view me as an ordinary, sane person and that the following story isn't a psychotic breakdown.

This story will seem hard to believe, but hear me out. This is all true. Every word of it. It cost me two and a half days of sleep, and I am certain that my mental stability was on the verge of snapping. By the end of this story, you will probably think I didn't have any mental stability beforehand.

Here is a word of caution: before you play the Blair Witch game, say a prayer, drink holy water, wear rosary beads—I don't know or care, but do something to protect yourself. The Blair Witch is real… and she's in the game.

Oh, and all the names of the children mentioned in this story are fake to hide their identities.

The game came out on August 30th this year, but I couldn't buy it until September 6th. After seeing it at E3, I was sucked into the idea of hunting down the Blair Witch in a game.

Everybody has seen the movie, so they should know the plot, but I'll explain it to the kiddies reading this.

In October of 1994, these college students travel to Burkittsville, Maryland to learn about the local legend about the Blair

Witch. They ask the locals about a hermit who lived in the woods and kidnapped eight children in the 1940s. The story goes that the hermit killed seven of those kids as a sacrifice for the Blair Witch.

They eventually go into the woods and are never seen again. The kids go missing, and the film footage is supposedly "found" during a search-and-rescue to locate them. The Blair Witch Project kicked off the found-footage film craze of the early 2000s.

I won't tell you anything else about it because I won't spoil anything if you're too young to have seen it back then—you really should watch it.

They never actually see the Witch, but the cinematography makes you think she's there with them, and some people swear to have caught glimpses of her in various shots.

I purchased the game digitally because I didn't feel like waiting for it to come in through Amazon Prime. It was a Friday night, and with no other plans, I intended to play the game until I passed out. After a couple of hours of downloading and about four beers, the game was ready, and I dove in. In the game, you play as Ellis, a former cop, who brings his German Shepherd, Bullet, to help find a missing boy. Over the radio, I heard, "Nine—year-old Mitchell Jenkins has been missing for four days. Police are actively searching for the young boy and are taking volunteers to assist the search in the Black Hills Forest."

It took a few seconds, but I realized something.

I have a student named Mitchell Jenkins in my class. "Weird," was all I could say. I didn't think much of it then, so I resumed the game. Ellis guided his Ford Bronco down the road, listening to the radio and eventually turning off into the forest, heading toward the place where the police were gathering for the search.

There were no police for the character to talk to, so I did the typical thing in a game and started searching the cars for clues. I found a picture of the missing boy and dropped my controller. It was my Mitchell, my student, not some imaginary kid created for the game.

The resemblance was startling. After reading various websites summarizing the game's story, I had to take out my phone. None of the websites mentioned the missing boy in the game as Mitchell Jenkins, except Peter Shannon. It just didn't make sense. Nothing made sense. The more I read about how Mitchell should not be in that game, the more panic set in. My mind began to calculate how this could be possible.

Was it some overly complicated prank? Probably not.

I have a brief idea of what video game programming is like, so this was deduced easily.

Was this a glitch in the game? Nothing on the internet mentioned this kind of issue or anything similar.

Did my download somehow corrupt? Nothing else seemed wrong with the game, so I doubted that.

Was it possible for the game to know things about my personal life and incorporate them into the game? This one didn't seem as farfetched as the rest. We all know that big tech companies track everything we do online, so I thought this possibility was the most logical. Perhaps this was a feature that most people hadn't discovered yet.

I decided to keep playing, and I'm glad that I did.

I had Ellis and Bullet search the other police cars. We found notes from the police about possible leads and a note from one of his former co-workers who was expecting him.

"Ellis, I know this is hard for you since Mitchell is one of your students, but try not to let AND EIGHTY POUNDS, WITH BROWN HAIR AND your emotions get the best of you. We are all here with you, all in this together. We will find him and bring him home."

The high-pitched shriek of an emergency alert coming from my actual phone startled me.

YOUNG MALE, AGE 9, NAMED MITCHELL JENKINS. MISSING FOR 48 HOURS. HE IS ROUGHLY FOUR FEET NINE INCHES IN HEIGHT AND EIGHTY POUNDS, WITH BROWN HAIR AND BROWN EYES. PLEASE CONTACT LOCAL LAW ENFORCEMENT IF FOUND OR IF YOU HAVE ANY FURTHER INFORMATION.

"Yep, that's Mitchell," I declared.

I wandered through the trees in Black Hills Forest, finding nothing but strange animal noises. After what felt like an hour of wandering, I found myself back at the parking spot.

Frustration and annoyance at the game for giving you no instructions to go, other than the clues you find, made me feel exhausted. I looked at my phone at the time.

2:30 am.

"Shit," it was much later than I thought it was. I rubbed my eyes, feeling the burn of sleepiness.

After completing my ritual of brushing my teeth and staring at my phone for a while, I drifted off to sleep.

I awoke at some point in the middle of the night. I didn't slowly come awake, but within a second, I was fully awake… and paralyzed. Nothing would move except for my eyes. I tried to speak, but no sound came out. I heard something shuffle at the foot of my bed.

Why is Dagger acting like that?

A blackened hand slapped onto the bed near my left foot, then another by the right. With a speed that seemed in slow motion, I watched a shadowed figure pull itself onto my bed. The weight of the figure on top of me made it difficult to breathe. The panic was flooding throughout me, but my body still did not move. The figure slowly crawled up to my face, then bent and whispered into my ear.

I am immortal.

You cannot stop me.

You cannot save the children. Kill yourself.

Kill yourself and avoid the torment to come.

Her breath reeked of rot and decay, making vomit bubble up my throat.

In a second, she was gone. My limbs regained movement, and I got off the bed. My sheets and clothes were soaked in sweat.

Instinctively, I checked my phone. 3:30 am.

I decided to shower, trying to rid myself of the stench of that figure's breath. As I was drying off, I felt something burn on my neck. I checked myself in the mirror and discovered a burn on my neck, like the human-shaped stick figures from the Blair Witch Project movie. The cut was red and angry, burning like I had been branded like a cow.

That proved to me that all of what happened was real.

Those words kept popping into my head as I attempted to go back to sleep.

I am immortal.

You cannot stop me.

You cannot save the children. Kill yourself.

Kill yourself and avoid the torment to come.

Thoughts of poor little Mitchell, scared and alone, would not leave my head. He's a quiet, loner kid who I sometimes forgot was even there, the type of kid to sit in a corner and read by himself rather than play with the other kids. Knowing that he was by himself with some psycho that would probably kill him angered me, made me want to hunt the bitch down and kill her. But notice she said "children." There were others. She had more kids to use for her devious desires.

The beep of the Xbox turning back on snapped me back to reality. I heard Dagger in the living room, whining like he was scared. I calmed him down by patting him on the head and reassuring him that nothing was wrong. I didn't turn the Xbox on. I don't know if the Witch was taunting me or if it was something else nudging me to it. My controller was powered off on the couch, so that couldn't explain how the Xbox came on. Shrugging it off, I continued the game.

Back at the parking lot, I decided to look for clues around the cars again. This time, I found two more photos of missing children from the area. Cassandra Holland and Milo Lawrence. Two more of my students.

Cassandra was an outgoing girl with a remarkably high intellect for a third grader, and Milo was a hyper kid who tended to be sporadic. From what I could tell, the Witch was nabbing kids at random with nothing in common other than they were all my students. Maybe that was the reason she was specifically targeting them. But why?

After searching for more clues in the cars, I found out all three disappeared on the same day. Mitchell's family said he was walking to a friend's house down the block. Cassandra was playing in their fenced-in backyard while her mother was tending to the flowers that lined the house. Cassandra's mother reported that they have a six-foot privacy fence that would be difficult for an adult, let alone a child, to jump. Milo's family said he was packing his bags to stay with his grandparents for the weekend when he just vanished from his bedroom. Milo's parents reported no windows were open, and it was a straight drop from the second floor to the ground, so that seemed unlikely. I just shook my head because I knew why.

A question popped into my head—were they trapped in the game? Had the Witch somehow made her way into the virtual world of the internet to steal kids? Was that even possible? If she were in there, that would mean she would have access to the millions of people that would buy the game.

I had to stop her.

Back in the game, I started traveling in the opposite direction that I began. Bullet, the main character's German Shepard, started going crazy and running toward an area directly ahead of us. In the brush, he led me to a pair of sneakers. I checked the reports for each kid, and these belonged to Mitchell. He took off again, and a few yards later, he found a dirty baseball cap that belonged to Milo. Not much further was a jacket that was Cassandra's. It was straight that these were all leading in a straight line. Common sense tells you it's a trap, but I assumed it was just part of the plot, so I kept going.

Up ahead, I found an old, rotted cabin located in the middle of a clearing. I could hear voices, but they were too far to decipher. Bullet took off as soon as we got into the clearing, charging straight into the old cabin. I ran over there, finding Bullet licking the faces of three happy, disheveled kids.

None of them would speak. They just stared at me, but it was as if they were looking through me and not at me. It took just a few moments of watching their dirty, maddened faces to determine that they were my students. They all sat in a circle on the floor, looking in my direction but not blinking or even moving.

"Kids? You okay? You've had everyone worried. I think it's time to go home. Kids?" not one of them responded or even flinched. I watched them for a few minutes, noticing they didn't even blink.

"Okay, kids. It's time we head back now," they cut me off. Their mouths opened in terror, but they didn't make a sound. Their little hands lifted, index finger extended, pointing directly behind me.

A chill crawled up my neck, goose pimples upon the overwhelming animalistic sense of fear that swarmed my mind.

A cut scene started.

Ellis turned, and the Witch floated a few feet above the ground, her black gown flowing in some ethereal wind that I couldn't feel. A long black hood obscured her face. She pointed back, cackling. Bullet ran at her, but he collapsed to the ground with a pained scream.

"Come, my children. Come to me. It's time that we go home."

Ellis screamed, "No!" and rushed the Witch. After a few steps, he stopped in his tracks and collapsed. Gasping for air, he clawed at some unseen hand that was trying to choke the life from him. Bullet was by his side, licking his face, confused at his master's pain. As he thrashed about, a crucifix that he wore around his neck fell out of his shirt. The Witch hissed in pain and relinquished her grip on Ellis.

Ellis led the kids back to the cars with Bullet on guard. All the cops who were there have now disappeared. He loaded them all into his Bronco and climbed into one of the police cars.

Finding a radio, he keyed up, "All units, this is Ellis Lynch. I have located all the missing children. They need medical attention. Anybody there?"

After a few agonizing moments, an answer came back; "We read you, Ellis. Are you in the parking lot at the entrance to the Black Hills Forest?"

"10-4. I will have them in my Bronco waiting for EMS."

The credits begin to roll. An ambulance arrives and examines the children. Ellis walks by himself to the edge of the parking lot, staring into the thick forest. Something catches his eye.

The Witch stood on the ground between some trees. I'm not done with you yet.

The credits kept rolling as the game ended. I looked at my phone.

1 pm.

I hadn't slept in twenty-nine hours. The exhaustion hit me then. I climbed into bed and dreamed the worst dreams I have ever endured.

The kids are all fine. They were discovered in the woods outside the town just hours after I finished the game. From what I was told, they were scared and had no idea how they got there. The police have stated that they are still investigating if there is a suspect in their disappearances.

Since then, I have been awakened repeatedly every night, dreaming that she is standing beside my bed and whispering threats. I also wake up with scratches, always in threes, in random places on my body. Dagger, my husky, won't come into my room at night anymore—the closest he will get is in front of the door.

I decided to write this as a warning to everyone. The Witch told me her plans for how she wants to use the game. She said that she would keep taking kids, and they would never be returned if you didn't succeed in the game. And she'll become increasingly powerful.

After that? I don't know.

But for the love of everything holy, don't play the new Blair Witch game.

THE FACELESS MAN

I PUT MY TICKET INTO the kiosk and went to the train steps. It was bitterly cold that day—a record-setting low. I bundled up tight in my knit scarf, the extra insulated coat I had bought the day before, and my ultra-warm gloves. The inside of the train car was cozy and warm, so I didn't hesitate to remove the thick clothing.

I was running.

I didn't have a car and couldn't afford a plane ticket. A train was the fastest, cheapest thing I could afford then.

What was I running from?

Outside the train window, I saw him. The faceless man in the wide-brimmed hat and overcoat. He always hides in the shadows, and right then, he was lurking from behind a large support beam that held the station's roof.

What does he want?

I have no idea, but he always waves, beckoning me to come with him.

I really don't want to know where.

I'm just hoping he doesn't follow me this time.

REVENGE IN WHITE

I SAT BY THE FIRE, TRYING to keep my hands from freezing. The bitter winds blew through the cracks of the old cabin, and you could see frost building up around the windows. I picked the wrong damn time to go there, that's for sure. The logs cracked and popped as I prayed the small stack of wood would last me until this storm died. Beside me, the fire glowed off the pallid skin of her corpse. Thankfully, her meat cooked well on the fire so I could feast in peace and quiet for a weekend; I had plenty more left to keep me alive.

She was a dumb, loud-mouthed bitch, and she ran that mouth up until I planted the hatchet into her thick skull. She kept yelling and thrashing around while I dragged her up the mountainside to my favorite kill spot. God, it was so satisfying to shut that trap of hers. Her body flopped to the ground and rolled around a bit like my victims usually do from a swift blow to the head.

I don't like that because of the mess they make, but what the fuck? The messier it was, the more satisfying it felt to shut her up. It had been a while since I had killed, and I had to rid myself of the itch somehow. I brought her up to my cabin so that I could feast in the peace and quiet of isolation for the weekend.

The wind was fierce, sometimes blowing hard enough to rattle the entire cabin. Occasionally, I could swear that I would hear words coming with the wind. At first, I thought it was isolation and my stupid brain picking up words out of silence, but it became increasingly obvious. At first, it was only whispered, but it became louder once the wind picked up.

"Frank. Frank. Frank," it would say, droning out each word, almost as if it were moaning. The harder the wind whipped, the louder the words were.

"Don't you remember us, Frank? Don't you remember us?"

Maybe I was going insane, I thought. Maybe I had finally grown a conscience and felt terrible for my actions. Nah. Never. I was just going fucking insane. Finally! I knew it would happen someday.

"Remember what?" I answered back. Yep, I had officially gone totally fucking crazy.

"Remember killing us, Frank. I'm sure you do. I'm sure you savored the sexual climax you get when you cut our throats, bashed our heads in, and shot us in the deep forests while you fondled yourself over our corpses. That, I'm sure you can remember well."

"Sure do. What do you want?"

"We're coming for you, Frank."

Yeah, I'll admit it—I panicked. I got up and ran over to my backpack and found my .45. In a frantic mess, I waved it around.

"Show your fucking self! Come on! I'm not afraid of you! Who's out there? Why are you fucking with me?"

"We're not here yet, Frank, but we will be. It won't be long," the voice said as it trailed off in laughter that sounded like a crowd cackling in unison.

I ran into the master bedroom and locked the door with the old iron key that came with the place. Nothing was to come into that room and make it out in one piece. The dresser was nearby, so I shoved it in front of the door. Keep in mind that I haven't had proper military training or anything, so I cowered in the corner with my pistol pointed at the door. It wasn't long before the door started rattling.

"Frank," the voice behind the door called as it fumbled with the doorknob. Now, I could tell that it was the voice of a woman. The voice sounded familiar. "Do you remember my voice, Frank? My body is in front of the fireplace. Surely, you can remember I screamed at the top of my lungs as you dragged me by my hair through the mud and rocks up the path. You remember taking me to that spot miles into the woods, far away from prying eyes or ears that could hear me screaming for help?" It started ramming the door. The dresser budged just slightly with each thump.

"Frank, no matter what you do, we will get you. All of us. We are all here. Nothing will stop us from seeking revenge for what you did to us," the voice informed me as it rammed the door.

The thing behind the door stopped, then gave one great heave, shoving the door wide open. The dresser flew across the room into the wall, leaving a hole where it hit. In the doorway stood the partially eaten corpse of the woman I had killed earlier that day. Behind her stood several other mangled corpses, all ranging from slightly decomposed to I-don't-know-how-they-were-able-to-walk rotten. The stench reached me then—a gut-churning odor of rotten meat and decay.

At once, they all spoke.

"We told you we were coming, Frank. Now, it is time to pay. It's time to atone for all your sins."

The ones who could run did. The barely put-together bodies just shuffled as fast as they could. But they were on me in no time. I watched as they chewed and pulled at my flesh, felt them devour my innards and my meat, and heard them moan with intense pleasure as the taste of my body touched their starved and insatiable palates. That was the last thing I remember.

I woke up in a hospital bed, my arm handcuffed to the bed.

An officer was sitting next to my bed, and when he saw that I was awake, he stood up.

"Mr. Frank Russo. You are under arrest for the murders of nine women."

"What? What are you talking about? How did I get here?"

"I'm not surprised you don't remember. A park ranger found you passed out in the snow, nearly frozen to death. They found a note in your hand, a handwritten confession to everything you had done."

I sighed. "They got their revenge, all right."

"What was that?"

"Nothing. Just take me in and I'll confess. I'll tell you everything."

After the doctor cleared me to leave, they drove me to the station, where I told them *everything*. It was time to seek atonement for everything I had done. Once I was finished, the officer taking notes looked up at me.

"Is that all?"

"Well, as I was passed out in the snow, I had a dream they all came back to life and ate me. Funny shit, right? I guess I do have a conscience."

The officer stared at me with confusion. "Mr. Russo, you do know that we found bite marks all over your body. The doctors wondered how you got that many, but we paid little attention to it."

I paused, lifting my shirt. They were all over my stomach and chest—bite marks, human bite marks. They weren't very deep, like maybe something a toddler could do. I screamed, "What the fuck?"

"That's exactly what we were wondering," the officer said as he sipped his coffee. "One more thing. Did you fight someone in your cabin? We found this huge hole in the wall from what appears to have been a dresser thrown into it. Mr. Russo?"

I fainted then. The shocking confirmation that what happened to me was not only real, but left evidence to back it up. I am sitting on this bunk, writing all this down to keep myself sane and document what has happened to me since. I still dream about those women. They haven't left me alone. They return every night. Either in my dreams or they wake me from my slumber, repeating the stories of what I did to each of them, reminding me of the pain and suffering they endured at my hands. And the worst part?

They tell me that they are still hungry, and I wake up each morning as they start consuming my flesh. I can only imagine what will happen when it comes my time to die.

I THOUGHT YOU WERE DEAD

DAY 1

This will be my journal detailing my recovery from the death of my wife, Wendy. Dr. Young insisted that I do this and that it would be helpful. Maybe I'll publish this online someday? This is my first day, so pardon me if this rambles on and on.

Do you know what the hardest part has been? Packing away all her things.

I went through all these memories, trying not to cry and failing while stuffing them into cardboard boxes to be put in the attic for God knows how long. I recall thinking, "I'm packing away Wendy into these little boxes," and breaking down in tears, crying so hard that I couldn't find the strength to get off the floor. That's how my days have gone.

Rinse. Repeat.

When Wendy died, so did my happiness. I've been finding random items in the closet—like the teddy bear I won for her on our first date at the carnival in 2005. She was so happy then, giggling with such merry delight that it was like she had just won a car instead. She said, "I've never won anything before!" and I replied, "Well, it's yours then!"

She hugged me tight, and we were inseparable from that point on.

I can smile now, but then, as I boxed up all those memories, I just cried like a baby—my chin wrinkling, my eyes contorting, just pure ugly crying. Crying is not my thing, but sometimes, you have to just let it flow or you might explode from all the pent-up pressure. I sat there on the floor of our room, holding our fading wedding photo, crying so hard that I couldn't see. My eyes hurt, and a migraine was forming, but it just would not stop. It had been eight days since the funeral, and my younger brother, Matt, talked me into starting the process.

"Sean, you have to do it sometime. You can't just sulk the rest of your life. Wendy loved you, and you loved her. That will never change. It's a terrible truth, but you must untangle the vines, man. Break yourself free and move on from the past."

"I know, Matt. It's just hard." My tears were smearing down the face of the iPhone, but I couldn't care less.

"It'll be fine. Stay strong. I'm always here if you need to talk. Hell, I'm five minutes away, brother. I'll come over, and we can have a beer or twenty," he chuckled and nudged my shoulder, trying to get me to do the same. I only had the energy to give a light-hearted exhale.

"Thanks, little bro. I'm glad I have you around," I said as I nursed a glass of whiskey on the rocks.

There's a certain kind of pain that comes with loss, a pain that never goes away. It lingers and persists, always lurking in the back of your mind. The only thing that helped was the whiskey. It at least numbed the pain some. I know that's not the healthiest cure, but hey, man, I was desperate.

After I hung up with Matt, I kept packing. I tossed back the rest of that whiskey, felt the soothing burn go all the way down to my empty stomach, and ripped some more tape off the roll.

I heard a knocking at the door, almost like something from Poe.

I assumed it was Matt, so I took my time answering it. Then I realized it wasn't coming from the front door.

The knocking was coming from the other side of the bedroom door.

Knock.

Knock.

Knock. "Matt?"

My body froze, and my heart felt like it had dropped into my stomach. It was Wendy; that was Wendy's voice. *Who? What? How?* I thought. I scoured through all the possibilities, like maybe I was imagining it, or my brain was translating a squeak from the house settling as her voice. Maybe it was even possible that I was going insane from all this.

"Let me in, hon. Your wife is home once again. Isn't this what you wanted?" It was definitely not the usual sounds of an old house—that was undoubtedly her voice.

"C-come back for me?"

"Yes, baby. I'm going to take you with me. We are going to start all over again like this never happened." She sounded eager and excited about this, like she had the best news of my life.

The whiskey wasn't helping, so I decided to drink more, this time straight from the bottle. After a hardy gulp, I replied, very much beginning to fear something else was going on, "I don't want to die, Wendy. I'm not ready."

"But you said you couldn't live without me, right?" I knew she was trying to get into my head. She was always good at that, almost expert level, playing those guilt trips. Matt had warned me for years that she was playing me, but I never saw it that way. Even when I discovered she had cheated, I found it easy to forgive her. I must be a gullible fool, right? By the end, I could see through her, and I was preparing to leave her for good.

"I also said, 'til death do us part, and I sure did."

"Quiet, Sean. Now listen. I know you blame yourself for what happened, but it wasn't your fault." I hated her tone.

Nobody used that tone except Wendy or my mother, and only when they were angry or condescending.

"It is, and I know that it is, Wendy.

"Look. The elevator was broken. I was in a rush because we had reservations at that fancy Italian place. What was the name? Del Tony's, or something. Anyway, I fell, baby. I fell down the steps because I was rushing. I broke my neck on the way down. It's not your fault."

I filled my glass with more whiskey, wishing I had some ice, tossing back some of it. "It is, and I accept that," drinking some more, "I'm not going to fall for your lies again, Wendy."

"Shut up, Sean. You were always so whiney and self— loathing. Look at you, drinking away your pain. Pathetic. I almost don't want to take you with me."

"I don't want to go. I am going to stay right here. In fact, I'm glad that you're gone. All you did was yell at me and fuck other men! Go away!"

"Please, open the door, Phillip. I'm sorry for all of that. I am! I want to hold you again. I need to! We can make it work this time! It'll be just like the good old days!"

My anger from remembering all the deception I had fallen for began to subside. My loneliness and the sadness of losing my wife overwhelmed me. Almost as if something else was controlling me, my arm as I opened the door, and I wish that I hadn't. I saw this graying, rotted thing with a crooked neck that used to be my wife. Her lips were still that ugly painted red that the funeral home drew on her, along with the bad makeup.

"Hug me, baby."

That was when I fainted.

Day 2

I accept that I've never been the toughest person on Earth, but seeing what my wife had become would take down the strongest people. When I did wake up, the bottle of whiskey was on the floor next to me; the contents spilled across the carpet.

My cat, Milo, was prancing around the room, inspecting last night's events.

"Yeah, I know, Milo. Another rough night. I know. You don't have to nag," I said while trying to soak up the alcohol with an old shirt I left on the floor.

Depression does odd things to you, like not bathing for days, not cleaning up after yourself and leaving dirty clothes in random places, and forgetting to eat. Unfortunately for me, it can also make you drink.

My phone said it was three in the afternoon by the time I was done. Work had given me two weeks off and paid me to recuperate, so thank God for that. I had thirty-five texts and fifteen phone calls waiting for me as well. All of my family were checking on me. I'm thankful for all of them, but damn, is that annoying when fighting off a righteous hangover.

I replied to all of them with.

'I'm fine. Everything's good here. Not dead.'

It's funny now that I chose to say that. Not dead. Wendy surely wasn't. She was coming after me, like a hungry dog after fresh meat. I'm not even sure that is Wendy. Something didn't seem right about her.

The hangover was ripe by then as well. I walked into the kitchen, holding my head and groaning. The dull throb was pounding a thousand nails into my head every second that ticked away. As I dug through the medicine cabinet for the bottle of Excedrin, I got a text from Matt. The letters were distorted, and the room danced before me as I read it.

'Coming over after work tonight. Probably around seven. I'll bring the booze.'

I wanted to reply with, 'Great, more booze is exactly what I need. Thanks, bro.' But I resisted. Instead, I sent, 'See ya then.'

I checked all my social media while sipping on some brewed coffee. I hadn't posted a single thing about Wendy, yet I had so many fucking 'sending prayers' posts on my wall that I wanted to puke and could have, considering everything. I thought, 'Pray to who? The being who allowed this to happen?

The being who allowed me to be with such a terrible person for so many years? The being that has allowed me so much pain?'

"Baby?"

I looked around and saw no one, but I knew instantly that was Wendy's voice.

"Baby, he's going to find out."

"Find out what?" I said out loud to the disembodied voice, like that's a totally sane thing to do.

"Find out that I'm back. They will make me leave. I can't stay if they find me, Sean."

"I didn't know you were staying?"

"I am until I convince you to go with me."

"I'm not going…"

"Go upstairs. I'm bathing. It's nice and hot. Come join me."

I hate to admit it, but my curiosity was peaked. I didn't want to see my dead wife bathing, but something stirred inside of me, and I couldn't resist the chance. Slowly opening the door, I looked inside. If I saw that gray thing in my bathtub, I was calling an exorcist or finding a way to contact one.

"I know my previous appearance didn't please you, Sean. I had a suspicion you'd like this one *much* better," her voice smooth as velvet and seductive.

I don't know how, but she was nineteen again. Her red hair was long again, her big, perky breasts were barely under the water, and her long, pale legs stretched to the faucet, the bubbles teasing me with what was under the water—all of that was enticing me to join her.

"Wendy…"

"Shush, Sean. Come on in. It's hot and wet in here, just like I am."

"You hate how I like my baths."

"I'll do anything for you now, baby. Anything. You name it. I wasn't the best wife before, but now I will be. Second chances, right?"

"Yeah, second chance, all right."

I sighed, but found little reason to not take my clothes off and climb in. If this were just some incredibly realistic whisky dream, then I would take it as far as it would go. She pounced on me not as soon as my butt entered the water. Her tongue slipped deep into my mouth. It was warm and vivacious, not rotten like I had feared. I grabbed her thick breasts and found them firm and lively. It didn't take long for an erection to rouse.

We had the most amazing sex in that bathtub. I can't remember ever being that satisfied. I was exasperated and drained of every ounce of energy. Her luscious coercion practically hypnotized me. I would take it as far as it goes.

"You can keep me here," she said, stroking my hair as I rested my head on her chest. "I can be your secret, and we can fuck like this every night if you want. I'll do whatever you want. You can even cum in my mouth."

"I thought you hated that? Doesn't that make you sick?"

"I'll do anything for you, Sean. We can even try anal," she said as she teased me by running her fingers under my chin. "Matt will be here in a few hours. Don't let him discover anything about us. I don't want to leave you again, Sean. Don't you want me to stay so you can have me whenever you want?"

"Yes."

"There is only one way to guarantee I'm never found, Sean. You'll have to kill him. Matt can't see me, Sean. Kill him. I don't care how, but kill him—then I can stay as long as you want."

"Whoa, wait a second…" I tried to counter, but she planted those soft, pouty lips on mine.

"Do as I say," she said as we made love again.

Matt's car pulled in just as I was pulling out. The only way that I can describe it is that I lost control of my body. My hands and legs moved without me wanting to. It was like riding in the passenger seat of a car driven by a maniac. I could only watch as my hand reached for a hammer from the utility closet, stuffed it into the back of my jeans, and waited by the front door for Matt.

"Hey, bro! I brought your favorite! Wild Turkey season is here!" he said, laughing as I let him in.

"Awesome! Exactly what I needed! Just put it in the kitchen. I'll be in there in a second."

He was shuffling through the bag to take all the stuff out when I slammed the claw end of the sixteen-ounce hammer into the back of his head with a sickening, wet, gushing sound. The claw bit into his skull with a wet thump. He hit the floor and started seizing, and my foot went down on his throat to hold him still. He flopped around the floor for a few minutes, his eyes rolling back and forth in his head, his teeth clinched down on his tongue so hard that it was nearly bitten off. Blood spewed out of his mouth in fountains as his body tried to breathe while he slowly suffocated to death. Eventually, he stopped moving, and I blacked out of consciousness.

Day 3

I woke up the next morning in my bed, not remembering any of the previous night. I walked into the kitchen to find Matt's corpse lying on the floor in a massive pool of blood and a broken claw hammer implanted claw first in the center of the gash.

I fell on my knees and could only cry in violent sadness, "Why did I do this? Why?"

"You did a good job, baby! Good job, my precious, amazing, devoted husband! I am *so* happy! Now we can be together *forever*!" she spoke inside my head.

"No!" I screamed out loud, "I don't want to be with you forever! I don't want my brother dead, and I don't want a corpse for a wife! Go away!"

"No, Sean. You see, I can't go away." She said, walking around the corner from the living room into the kitchen. She was still nineteen and naked. "I can't go without you, Sean. I have to take you with me, but I can't force you. You must do it of your own free will, and I *will not* leave until I get what I want."

"No! Go away!" I screamed as I threw random objects at her. Nothing seemed to faze her, even when the toaster connected directly with her collarbone. She just stood there, grinning menacingly.

"You're coming with me, Sean," she said, slowly walking toward me through Matt's spilled blood. She bent down, wiping some of the blood up with her index finger. She licked it off seductively, taking an exceedingly long time for her tongue to move down her finger. "Mmmmmm. It's so tasty! The blood of an innocent! It's enough to make me… ohhhhhhh mmmmmm…" she moaned, "Don't you want me to keep this body forever, Sean?"

She backed me into the corner of the counters, and I slumped onto the floor, pointing at a steak knife that I snatched from a drawer.

"I thought you were dead! You're supposed to be dead! Why did you come back? Why?" I was crying by then. Fear does that to you.

"Because Sean, I need you. I *need* you! I *want* you!"

I blacked out again, waking up days later in a hospital bed with my arm handcuffed to the bed.

I found out later that I was going to be arrested for the murder of my brother after the hospital released me. I told them my story, told them every part of it, even about my dead wife coming back from the grave and what happened in the bathtub. The jury didn't take long to conclude that I was insane from grief, and the judge agreed. A psychiatrist analyzed me during the trial and said that I had developed psychotic delusions as a result.

They don't believe what I endured, though. No one does. I will be trapped in this asylum for the remainder of my life. They allowed me to write sometimes because they decided I was safe enough to use only markers.

Every day, I can hear her calling for me.

"Sean. Come with me, baby. Come be with me forever." It's always fucking there in my head.

Sometimes, I even see her standing outside the windows, completely nude, regardless of the weather, and watching me— with a smile stretching her mouth just a little too wide, waving for me to follow.

It's hard to ignore that and not let it bother me, but the meds do help with that. I can tune it out, sometimes long enough for her to give up. Eventually, though, she comes back.

I have concluded that my only escape is suicide. This is the only way that Wendy can take me with her. Either that or I when I die from old age. I can't imagine seeing and hearing her for that many years. I'm only thirty-five now. How many years do I have left? Thirty? Forty? Maybe fifty?

I've thought about all of this and played with the options in my mind for countless hours. I could break a mirror, jam the shards into my wrist over and over until I hit the artery, and hopefully bleed to death before an orderly gets to me. Or I could sit by and wait for Father Time to age me and the Grim Reaper to find me. I don't want to die, though, because I have a feeling that where she is taking me won't be a good place.

Matt, I am so sorry for what happened. I'm so sorry. I would've never killed Matt. It was Wendy—she made me do it! Her sex somehow let her control me, and she treated me like a murderous puppet. Ultimately, that's all I ever was to her—a plaything.

Matt, I hope you can forgive me for never listening to you.

Right now, though, I'm afraid I'll have to do what must be done.

LARGE YELLOW EYES

MY NAME IS JOHN DAWSON, and I served as a beat cop for twenty-two years in a small town in rural West Virginia. People talk, and stories get around quickly, especially in small towns with few ears and big, bored mouths. Sometimes the people knew a crime was going to happen before it would, and I was often warned to patrol certain houses for a while; most of the time, nothing happened, but they usually wound up being a domestic disturbance, such as two drunk men getting into a fistfight over a woman. I never took their foreknowledge as a psychic thing. Still, just people who knew other people so well that they could spot the signs or hear people announce their intentions for the entire town to hear. Then the nosy old ladies with nothing better to do would be the first ones to summon us.

"I heard that Barry Cook and Denver Thomas will duke it out by Bo Peep's after their shift in the mines. Barry said he might even bring his pistol!" something like that.

'Barry' usually left his pistol at home and only showed up bearing fisticuffs and a staggering disposition.

Now that you understand some of how small-town gossip works, I will explain to you the oddest thing I ever had to investigate. This changed my life forever. It's very difficult to find the words when you're talking about trauma, and this I know well from years on the force. Seeing the corpses of people you know, like friends and family, is bad in and of itself, but this was something else. You'll have to read my story first.

The night started as another boring summer night. I was patrolling the roads aimlessly, hoping to maybe stop a drunk driver from killing someone, watching for speeders, or some other random event, when the radio blared. It made me jump a little because I had it turned up after I had pulled off the road to take a leak by a river earlier that night and forgot to turn it back down.

"Unit 512. Are you close to Dempsey's? Over."

"10-4. What's going on? Over." I said as I juggled the mic, nearly dropping it to the floor.

"Neighbors have reported someone or something prowling around the building. Possible 459, or maybe a bear. They said they don't know but won't feel safe until someone looks."

459 means burglary. Oh, joy. I was hoping for some teenaged punk causing mayhem around town, not some armed, desperate lunatic trying to break into a business at two in the morning. I drove over that way and searched around the building. In the grassless mud, I saw some enormous paw prints. They were bigger than my palm. Coyote prints aren't nearly that big, and wolves have been extinct in this area for over one hundred years now. Maybe the coyote had sunk in the mud a little, so the print spread out, but it didn't appear that way. I'm not a good tracker, but I can tell a bear print from a dog, and this was a canine print to me.

"Station, this is Unit 512. All clear of a possible 459. There is no sign of entry and no alarms going off. Over."

"10-4, Unit 512. Over."

I did not mention the tracks I found, but it stayed in mind. What could make prints that big? The caller must've thought it was a human. I don't believe they would have bothered calling the police over some animals sniffing around a building. I returned to my aimless wandering of the roads and got some food from a fast-food joint while thinking about those huge dog tracks. I thought about maybe contacting the DNR later about a possible rogue wolf.

I parked by an empty car wash, watching coal trucks and pedestrian vehicles amble by occasionally. I saw a flash running by the passenger side door from my peripheral vision while I ate my dinner and occasionally flashed my radar gun to scare the local drivers into being safe. From my peripheral vision, I saw a flash running by the passenger side door. Beside me, there was the vast empty car wash parking lot that eventually led to a side street. I looked around and didn't observe anything out of the ordinary. I turned and looked out the driver's side door to see the biggest wolf that I could ever imagine. It was sitting on its haunches and staring at me. After a few seconds, it ran off behind the car wash, heading toward the woods. After I regained control of myself, I threw the car into the drive, peeling off onto the road and burning rubber to get away from it.

I have been shot at before. The most distressing time was when a drunken redneck, hell-bent on getting revenge on his wife's lover, shot at me for trying to stop him. That didn't even frighten me as much as seeing that wolf. When you see something you know isn't an illusion or a trick of light, your brain has trouble accepting it. It awakens something primal in your brain that humans don't have to use in modern society. Something urged me to get away from it, and I did. I drove around for hours, half-expected this *thing* to run out from the woods in front of my headlights.

I cruised past an active coal mine when my radio went off again.

"Unit 512. There's a 10-57 over at 22 Brooks Lane. Can you be over there in five? Over."

10-57 means missing person. It was turning into a night for the record books.

"Give me about ten. I'll be there as soon as I can. Over."

On came the red and blues, and down went the accelerator.

When I got there, I found a man and woman standing on the porch of their old coal camp house. The woman was crying with such fervor that I knew I wouldn't get much from her. The man was pacing; he was clearly distraught as well.

"Evening, folks."

The man walked down and introduced himself as the husband. He shook my hand; his palm was shaking and clammy.

"It's my daughter Cassie. My wife checked on her before bed, and Cassie's window was open. Some of the stuff in her room was knocked around like there was a struggle. Neither of us heard anything. She never opens her window. I can't understand how this could happen!" I was writing all of this down in my notebook as he spoke.

"I'd like to go look around if that's okay with you."

"Yeah. Sure. Not a problem, officer. Do whatever you need to."

In the room, I found large claw marks under the window.

You could tell from the pattern that this happened as it climbed in and back out. The window was about ten feet off the ground as the home was elevated due to frequent flooding. Her toys were knocked around, and her bedding was essentially shredded. It was as if someone had taken a sword and just sliced her bedding a thousand times. In disbelief, I stared. This was about five miles from where I had seen the wolf, but it was the first thing that popped into my head. I couldn't help but ask.

"Well, without a doubt, some animal got in here. Did you hear any growling or howling?"

"Ya know, I did. That happened earlier tonight. I just thought it was one of my neighbor's huntin' dogs, so I didn't think much of it. What in the world do you think it was?"

"Not sure yet, maybe a bear because of the claw marks on the bed and window. I'm going to have some more people come by and look. If Cassie ran away, do you know where she would go for safety?"

We yammered on for a while. Afterward, I radioed the sheriff about sending deputies to check where Cassie might've gone and about calling the local Search and Rescue team to scour the woods while the forensics team checked her room. About a couple of hours later, the small forensics team left. They found strands of thick, gray hairs around the room, but no blood. They also told me they thought it was an animal, but they needed more evidence to call it that officially.

I had about three hours left of my shift, and there was still no sign of Cassie, so I went back to driving. I had hoped that I might come across her by patrolling the roads. I even told the sheriff I would work over to help find her. I was driving along a section of town that used to be part of a coal mining community around the early 1900s. Many houses are now dilapidated and left to rot by the retreating, foreign-interest coal companies. I was driving by one home when I saw something out of the corner of my eye. The brakes on my patrol car screamed when I realized what it was.

In between two abandoned houses, I saw the wolf sitting on its haunches with an unconscious girl in its jaws, grinning. That grin didn't appear to be an animal grin—it was human, a human who was proud of itself. My instinct was to give chase, regardless of if it was a beast or a man. With my Beretta out, I went after that thing. I've never seen anything run so fast. In a flash, the wolf was up an old oak tree. I didn't want to shoot because it had the girl, and she might still be alive.

"Cassie!" I screamed, hoping it was her. "Are you okay?" I yelled up the tree.

"No, she's not." Said a gravelly voice back to me. The wolf had laid her down on some branches as it decided to talk.

Startled, I shouted, "You're human?"

"Oh yes. Yes, I am. This meal will fill me for a while, too, Officer Dawson. I can't wait. I'm practically starving."

From the top of the tree, it picked up Cassie into his clawed arms and leaped across the backyard onto the hillside, bolting toward the peak. I fired three rounds, but all of them were missed. It didn't take long for the wolf to climb the mountain and be out of sight. Several yards from the car, I grabbed my cell phone and called the station. I didn't want the public to hear what I was about to say.

"You're not going to believe this! I just saw Cassie! She was in the jaws of some wolf-like thing!"

"Wolf-like thing?" the station officer asked. "Yes! It spoke to me, and it knew my name!"

"Dawson, there's no way.."

"I'm telling you, it did! It went up the hill behind some abandoned houses near the old Campbell Mine Camp!"

"I'll radio the state police for a helicopter out there ASAP. As for the wolf, I'll pretend I didn't hear that. For your sake," he said as he hung up.

They sent a helicopter out, and they did find the girl. She was mostly devoured; just bones remained from the chest down; the rest were never found. The funeral was the roughest I have ever been to. The entirety of our small police force attended, and we saluted the girl as she was sent off to the great beyond. My wife hand made them a picture frame with multiple pictures of Cassie. She was Cassie's homeroom teacher and was absolutely destroyed by what happened. It's been five years and I still don't think she's completely over it, and she probably never will be.

Another event occurred over a week later. The Sheriff gave me a paid week off over the few days prior. The events of the vicious murder of Cassie had finally started to simmer down. I cruised through the business section of town a little after midnight, checking the front and back sides of businesses for anyone attempting to break in.

"Unit 512. Come in. Over."

"This is Unit 512. Go ahead. Over."

"Got a possible 187 down on the far end of Miller Hollow. A driver said they thought they saw a body in the ditch but didn't want to investigate. Over."

A 187 means murder. Dead body. Great; it's a good way to start things off after my mini vacation. The amount of paperwork that follows one of those is ridiculous.

"10-4. I'll go over that way now. Over." I admit I was anxious, but I had a job.

I went to the approximate area. I searched down the road, and they said the body was spotted, and I found it. The body was covered in deep slashes. And to top it off, the head was missing. I shined my flashlight around, trying to find a sign of what might have happened or the head. Several yards up the hillside, I saw a tall, naked man grinning at me. His body was partially covered in long, gray hair. He ran up the hill, and I never saw him again.

The creepiest thing about him was his large yellow eyes.

A COLD, DEAD BODY

IT WAS THE SUMMER OF 2004, the summer when we found the dead body of Fred Ames. When you grow up in a small town, anything other than the normal, boring routine is considered adrenaline-rushing, heart-pumping, excitement. We occasionally heard about dead animals, like when Tommy Smalls told us about a dead deer on the riverbank near his house. We decided to investigate the rumor. A flurry of rats exploded from the corpse when Shawn threw a rock at it. The explosion also released the stink of decay, making us gag and nearly vomit. But the story I'm about to tell you is not like that.

This story is about the cold, dead body of Fred Ames, and it still haunts me to this day.

My friends and I were riding our bikes in the scorching heat of early July. As we passed Tommy's house, he saw us from his yard and came running over to us with all the speed his chubby fourteen-year-old legs could summon.

"Guys! Guys!" he was yelling breathlessly at us. It took him a few moments to catch his breath. "Ya know the old drunk, Fred Ames?"

"Yeah?" one of us replied.

"I heard that he was hit by a train a few nights ago, and Jeff said he saw Fred split in two. He said both parts were lying over the bank in the weeds. He said it was the most awesome thing he ever saw!"

It took us all three seconds to decide that we had to see this for ourselves. Tommy got his bike and followed us down the dirt path that followed the tracks that the railroad men used to inspect the tracks. After several minutes of riding the road, Tommy yelled, "There! That's where Jeff saw him!"

We threw our bikes down and ran up to the tracks. The four of us started to search, but it didn't take us long to find it. We followed the sound of the buzzing flies and the smell of decay to where his body lay. A small creek was at the bottom of the slope, where his legs lay partially. His torso was a few feet away, the organs flopped onto the ground like oversized earthworms. It was obvious that some animal had already started eating him by then. I watched as flies scurried across and into his open, lipless mouth and down in the holes where his eyes had once been.

Rigor mortis had frozen his hands into claws. The putrid stench of rotting flesh baking in the nearly one-hundred-degree heat was almost unbearable, even from the distance we were.

We stared for a few moments before someone finally said it. "Go touch it, Tommy!" Mark commanded.

"Fuck no! That stinks so bad I might puke! You touch it!" he said as he covered his nose.

"You're the one who told us about it!"

"I'm not touching that nasty ass thing! One of you do it! Remember the deer? No rat's gonna bite me! No way! It might explode if I touch it!"

"A rat bit nobody, Tommy," I informed him.

Shawn, the bravest one of us, and the one who exploded the dead deer, picked up one of the large rocks that lined the tracks and chucked it at Fred. The rock hit the corpse on the left set of ribs, and a hollow, meaty, bone-crushing crunch followed.

Followed by a gasp. We looked at each other, but the sound hadn't come from us.

The half-rotted head of Fred Ames slowly turned around, chest heaving slightly in low gasps of air.

"Helllllllp…. Meeeee…. Helllllllp… meeeeeeee…."

I remember that I could feel the blood leaving my face so fast that I was on the verge of fainting. We scurried back up the rocky slope, making a mess of tumbling rocks as we made our flight. Tommy was almost at the top when he slipped, causing rocks to tumble down and removing any grip for climbing back up. The rocks and Tommy all cascaded down the hill toward old Fred Ames, who was still calling, "Helllllllp…. Meeeeeeee…."

Tommy tried desperately to grab hold, to maintain control, and haul himself back up the hill toward us, but he couldn't do it. He slid down to Fred Ames, landing about a foot from his torso to Tommy's utter horror. I have never seen someone have such a look of pure horror as Tommy did that day. His face went as pale as a sheet, and his eyes bugged out so far that they could've popped from their sockets. He was frozen, staring into the rotten face of Fred, glaring into the empty holes where Fred's eyes had been, straight into the open maw hanging on by a few strands of tendons, with a tongue black as tar.

"Helllllp… Meeeeee…. I'm…. Hungryyyyy!" Fred lunged at Tommy and grabbed onto his right arm, trying to pull him down. Tommy screamed a blood-curdling scream of fear and terror as he kicked and yelled, "Get the fuck off of me! Get off me, asshole! Get off! Let go!" Fred was relentless, refusing to let go. His grip was like iron, maybe from rigor mortis. I looked at my friends, who were all frozen in fear and staring at Tommy's situation. I had an idea. "Guys! Throw rocks! Now! We have to help Tommy!"

From the tracks, Shawn, Mark, and I chucked one rock after another at Fred, trying not to hit Tommy. Dozens of rocks flew down, and most missed Tommy and Fred—one hit Tommy in the ribs, but one large rock that Shawn hurled hit Fred's skull, caving it in with a sick, wet thump. Fred finally let go and flopped onto the ground, slowly sliding into the creek, lifeless again. Tommy scurried up the hill; this time, he had no trouble finding a grip.

None of us had ever peddled that hard in our lives. Once we were back at Tommy's house, we told his mother about finding the body, but we had agreed to leave out the unbelievable details. His mom called the police and reported Fred Ames' body. Nobody had called 911 about poor old Fred Ames being hit by that train before her. I'm not sure if the conductor just didn't realize they ran him over or just decided not to mention it.

We never went back to that spot. We were all too afraid, but we felt easy thinking that he was gone now. Tommy later told us that Fred's grip was ice cold, even though it had been boiling that day; none of us could explain why or how Fred was still alive.

I have often wondered this many times over the passing years: what would've happened if Fred had managed to bite Tommy?

CAPTAIN, THEY'RE COMING FOR US

January 19, 2090

This is the log of Captain James C Reynolds of the USS Nikola Tesla. We are a crew of one hundred, along with three hundred colonists, set to inhabit the forgotten colony on Mars. As for posterity, Mars was abandoned in 2087 to focus on World War V, which tragically just came to a nuclear conclusion. As we flew from Earth, we saw the mushroom clouds dotting the once beautiful, sustaining planet. It is sad to know that everything that has existed for humankind is now obliterated due to a rampaging, brain-devouring fungi that we call the Brain Eater. It would quicker cause people to go insane before it finally devoured your brain enough to render you lifeless. You awaken with your human cognition, and the fungus has completely taken over your body.

We were forced to use this spacecraft from the 2020s for the mission as everything else had been scrapped, repurposed, or just destroyed by the countless barrages of bombs over the last few years. This scrap heap was found in an old forgotten hangar in Texas and was transported, in total secret, to the new Cape Canaveral near Corpus Christi. It was our only hope, the vessel capable of getting us to Mars.

The survivors on Mars have become self-sufficient and have succeeded in growing more than enough crops to survive. The crew, colonists, and I have been sent off on a secret mission by the last U.S. President to ensure we will continue the human race on Mars. With us is a large amount of fertilizer, seeds, several forms of animal life, and a massive hard drive filled with several petabytes of information to continue humans' history, science, and mathematics.

Today, we had a successful takeoff from Earth, with no prior test launch and very little, very quick preparation. There wasn't much choice. If Mexico or Canada caught wind of our attempt, they could throw a volley of missiles at our site. Thankfully, we had a skilled crew who could get us off the ground without exploding into a cloud of metal and body parts, and we were also thankful that no one shot us down in the process.

If all goes well, we are set to arrive on Mars in approximately three hundred days.

January 30, 2090

Two days ago, there were reports of noise from the storage compartments. I had commanded five men to investigate this. My councilors and I concluded that it must've been a fault in the craft and that there couldn't have been much too much damage— otherwise, we would have exploded from the force of takeoff. Yet, it was discovered that we were wrong. That was not what caused the sounds.

When we inquired, the guards reported finding ten men in the storage area. There was a short battle between the two of them, who managed to take the weapon from a young woman who had volunteered for the guards just a few days before and shot her point blank between the eyes. The remaining guards returned fire, killing those two men. The other eight stowaways surrendered without incident.

The guards discovered that the stowaways had removed some of the fertilizer. At the same time, we were busy trying to get the damn ship ready for takeoff, pulling enough to hide ten men indiscriminately. If we weren't in such a rush to get off the planet, I would have sent guards to check all the rooms thoroughly, but we were short on time.

We have them locked up in a sealed room as a makeshift prison, with cameras pointed at them constantly, and the only way for them to get out is from the control panel in the Executive Quarters. I feel it is most secure having the control panel in here; you'd need executive-level access to get in here, which very few people have: Me, the co-captain, the captain of the guard, and my wife. The room is sixteen feet by nineteen feet, with ample space for the eight stowaways. I fully intend on leaving them there until we arrive. We will treat them as prisoners until then.

February 3rd, 2090

Today was the first, and I hope, the last time this happened on our journey to the new home. Several colonists revolted and began to protest outside the Executive Quarters. It started with a handful of people filling the thirty-foot hallway leading to the guards' barracks and the security office. They began beating on the windows and screaming obscenities.

"Come out, ya fucking scumbag! Show us your ugly face!"

"We aren't going to Mars to live under a dictatorship! We left Earth a free people and are still free!"

"Free those prisoners! They mean no harm! They just wanted off that goddamned planet too!"

"Free the prisoners! Free the prisoners! Free the prisoners!"

I commanded the Captain of the Guard to explain to the protestors that these people were not assessed for Brain Eater and have not been cleared yet. Things soon got out of hand. The protestors refused that answer, becoming even more rowdy, and then one of the guards beat a colonist over the head with her baton after they started clawing her face. She was reported to have yelled obscenities back at the angry protestor before unleashing her frustration on their skull, killing them after a few hard blows.

The crowd rushed the guards, and two colonists died in the ensuing unrest. The guards had to resort to brutal force when five people attacked an inexperienced guard who was too busy panicking in a corner and was killed after the protestors took his weapons. The guards shot and killed two of the protestors that had killed the guard and injured several others before the crowds rushed in the other direction, and the uprising finally stopped.

For the last several hours, I have been watching the cameras. The colonists have been in their quarters since the uprising was quelled, and so far, they seem to have gotten that out of their system for now. There are no cameras in their quarters, and I'm beginning to worry about what may result if something else upsets them. I have commanded the guards to watch them closely for the next few days.

The feeling of the walls closing in has never felt stronger.

February 4th, 2090

As I enter this log, I am in utter fear for the lives of everyone aboard this ship. One of the doctors who was doing a routine examination of one of the guards' corpses from the stowaway incident noticed that they had a strange mutation. It didn't take long for the doctor to realize what it was.

"It's the Fungus! The Brain Eater! It's on the ship!" the doctor said as he burst into my office in an absolute panic.

"Calm down, Doctor Marion. Are you sure?"

"Do I look sure!?" he replied, frantically screaming. I looked into the crazed man's eyes and saw only the harsh truth in them.

"Which body was it, Doctor?"

"The guard that died. Sheila MacDougall. I tried to trace the contamination, and she was fine when the other doctors and I checked everyone on the ship after takeoff. It had to have been transmitted on the ship! Wasn't she one of the guards that captured the stowaways?"

"Yes, but none of them showed signs of infection."

"Come! Look at the camera, then! See for yourself! She is walking around there now! Twelve hours ago, she was dead as a rock, but now she's walking around! You saw her when they brought her back!"

One of my guards had already switched the camera on by the time we had turned to face the wall of screens. On it, you could see the woman pacing around haplessly as if she weren't sure what to do or where to go. Her once beautiful blonde hair was now a tangled mess from the dried blood that bathed her head after the incident. Through the mic, you could pick up a gurgling growl coming from her mouth. A few seconds later, her head darts toward the camera in a sudden moment of clarity. I remembered that she had these pretty dark green eyes before, but now they were bright yellow and piercing a hole through us, gazing madly, resembling more of a starving animal than a human.

"We... will... come... for... you...," the dead woman growled at us, "There... is... no... hope... Captain..." she said, now laughing deeply, "You... will... become... us... all... of... you.... will."

"There! Do you believe me now!?"

"Yes," I admitted, "but what happened to the two stowaways that were killed during the row?"

"I was upset when I found this out, but the guards disposed of them through an ejection bay without consulting any of us first. None of them had mentioned checking the dead men for the signs either, but I will say they were most definitely infected as well."

"Dammit! This is why we had everyone assessed before coming on! We need to start decontamination as soon as possible..."

"It's too late for that! Too fucking late! We should have checked every nook and cranny thoroughly before takeoff! We should have done many things before takeoff, but we didn't have time! That goddamned war! That goddamned world!" he started crying, "But now... now... we are doomed. We won't make it to Mars. We won't make it. We won't make it. We... won't... make... it. We... won't... make... it. We... won't... make... it."

That was when the girl on the camera said, "You... won't... make... it..." and the doctor changed his to that, too. They were in harmony, taunting us with what they said would be our fate. Both were smiling from ear to ear, drool cascading down their slack maws as they continued to mock me and my people for fleeing the infested Earth.

They both continued to repeat the last phrase over and over and over again, sending me into a panic of my own. It was the Brain Eater, and it was on this ship. I had to do something, and something fast.

I noticed then the strange coloring on the doctor's lips. It was lipstick. It clicked then; she had kissed him of Death and infected him. I suppose even an experienced war doctor cannot control their animal instincts.

After removing my sidearm and shooting the doctor point—blank between the eyes, I ordered one of the guards to dump the corpse out of an ejection bay and also to do the same with the girl. I watched on camera as the guards entered her room, her head exploding like a rotten tomato. The last image permanently frozen in my mind of the doctor is of those vicious yellow eyes that were locked onto mine and that drooling mouth of his wide open, baring his teeth in the way of a starving beast. He was in the final stage before death.

I watched on camera as the doctor's headless corpse floated through space. We had spent years together fighting in the Fifth World War and had grown close. I respected the man greatly, and this tore my heart out. In my quarters, I cried for his loss, cried for the man I had known so well and had been so close to, cried for the man who had saved my life after a bullet struck my leg, and I nearly bled out. He worked tirelessly to save me, a stranger then. My gratitude will never end.

I will miss him.

I also mourn for Sheila and her family. Her mother and father are on board. Sheila was just twenty-three years old. She was also studying to be a botanist on Mars. Sheila had a long life and career ahead of her and was now ended because of this disease. I wish we could have prevented this.

February 5th, 2090

Today, I made a fatal mistake. My stubborn, determined son had been arguing with me for days to get out of the Executive Quarters because he was bored and wanted to see the whole ship.

"Dad! Just take me out there! I want to see something else! I'm tired of being cooped up in this hole!" He is a strong-willed nine-year-old, that's for sure. For three days, he badgered me every time I was within reach.

After the incident with the doctor, the security team decided it was safe enough to escort him around with me at his side. We left around noon today and started with Quarter A. All the Living Quarters are identical: twenty-five rooms that can house up to four people each and a cafeteria at the back of the hallway; four quarters can house four hundred people, which puts us at maximum upon takeoff.

As we were heading down the hallway of Quarter B, a man stepped out of his doorway as we stepped in. Once we passed him, he lunged out at my son, somehow wedging his way around the two guards and forcing him to the ground. Within maybe two seconds, he did this and was trying to force his mouth onto my son's. He struggled, and my son screamed at the top of his lungs. The guards moved quickly by throwing a swift head kick, sending him reeling backward. I told them before that if anyone attacked us, to shoot immediately, and they followed that order.

We turned around and made our way back to the Executive Quarters. Martin went back to his room and hasn't said a word since. I attempted to check on him, but he didn't respond; he just kept his nose buried in an old comic book he brought along that I'm sure he has read at least a thousand times by now.

I hope this doesn't scar him for life. Your first encounter with death is never easy.

February 6th, 2090

Throughout the night, all hell broke loose on this ship.

It started at 3 am when one of the guards did his twice-hourly check on the prisoners. They were gone. The captain of the guard and I pulled the video recording, but someone disconnected the camera around the time this happened. It wasn't clear who'd done it.

"Oh shit. This isn't good. Not good at all," the Captain of the Guard began to say as he panicked. He raked his fingers through his hair and paced around the room.

I don't feel it was a bad decision to fire him and immediately have him checked out for the Brain Eater. He was infected. He was also present during the investigation of the storage bay, confirming it had rooted back to the stowaways. To my dismay, I discovered that he was the one who had approved for them to dispose of the bodies without inspection. He was quoted to have said, "I don't want any fucking paperwork about this, so just throw them out the tubes. If they're infected, that'll stop them from spreading it."

One of his subordinates retorted, "Sir, what if they haven't been infected yet? There is that possibility…"

"Do as you're told, officer!"

It's a shame nobody in that group had the gall to stand up to that idiot.

I wish there had been time to screen everyone and tell them I had appointed a leadership position appropriately. Still, we didn't have the time again, just like how we went through six presidents in a year due to incompetence on all levels of leadership. I appointed people with good resumes who seemed competent during the quick interview process. None were chosen before takeoff, but I had done all this during the first day.

It seems that I am the only competent one on this goddamned ship. I feel a major shift in leadership is coming, and I think there may be a need for a drastic executive decision very soon.

February 8th, 2090

I have stood my ground, and I have stood it well.

The Captain of the Guard turned on us during our meeting. "I am not infected! You all are full of shit! This whole fucking ship is going to crash because you don't know what you're doing!" the Captain had yelled at me.

"You ought to watch your mouth before you swallow all your fucking teeth, Captain," I replied, my fist balled up so tight that my nails were nearly puncturing the skin of my palm.

"I know it will! I know it will! I.... know... it... will..."

It was that quick. The man's head did this strange movement of turning from side to side for a few moments, blinking rapidly, then he snarled and growled, and, in an instant, he leaped off the bed, attaching his mouth to the mouth of the doctor that had examined him. The poor man didn't see it coming.

One of the guards shot him and the doctor right then and there, no questions asked. The echo of the gun blast made me lose all hearing for a time, but it was a good move on the guard's part, and I commended him later. I like that kind of initiative that would make a good Captain of the Guard one day. Maybe soon, at this rate.

Upon finding out the Captain of the Guard was infected, I had the remaining doctors do an emergency examination of all the colonists and crew members. At the same time, I also had the guards search for the missing prisoners. No, they're not prisoners now, not even stowaways; they are terrorists. They are enemies of humanity! They brought the infection onto this ship, our last hope! They, or the fungi swimming around in their brains, know what they are doing well. It is programmed in the fungi to find more hosts, and they must have found out about our mission to get the hell of Earth before it was blown to Swiss cheese.

To my horror, the doctors found out that over eighty people had become infected, all of whom were immediately executed and discarded via the ejection pod. I watched the cameras as they slowly floated into the vacuum of space. I felt a strange mixture of sadness to see a little more of humanity's hope fly out of those pods, but I also immensely enjoyed seeing those infected people floating far away from the ship.

I spent the last three years fighting this fucking disease as it ravaged the world, turning everyday people into savage, murder-ous monsters. The disease is transferred by mouth-to—mouth contact only. Many times, I nearly faced the Kiss of Death, but I could fend it off with proper training and sheer determination not to become of them. It's not a kiss, but the infected lock their lips onto the host and fill the victim's mouth with their infected saliva until they are forced to swallow, rapidly spreading the spores throughout their system—sometimes in just a few minutes. The world was in deep shit when world leaders started to succumb to the disease and began to command entire armies of the infected, marching into countries and infecting millions. It was found out early on what the goal of the infected was—they didn't want to eradicate the human species; they wanted to become it.

When you are infected, your eye's sclera turns a piercing yellow, so it is easy to tell who has it. They can still operate like ordinary people, but their voice dramatically changes, sounding like they are trying to speak with a mouth full of water. They come after you in a bloodthirsty rage if you refuse the Kiss. They will scream and lash out like maddened animals, all to take you down and force you to become one of them.

God help us if they manage to get hold of the guns on this ship.

February 9th, 2090

The guards found the terrorists shortly after I filled out my log yesterday. They were found, blended in among the colonists. Since we have no Captain of the Guard, I assumed that role as well, for the time being, commanding the guards to execute them upon discovery and dispose of their bodies immediately. They did as commanded without hesitation. The people became outraged again, starting another uprising. These guards were quickly overpowered, had their weapons taken from their hands, and were murdered by the rampaging crowd.

All hell had broken loose once again.

As of today, we no longer have doctors; they have all become infected and are floating around the space between Earth and Mars, along with roughly one hundred others they were able to identify before it was too late. We now estimate that over fifty percent of the remaining colonists and crew have been infected.

I ordered the remaining guards to separate the non-infected from the infected forcibly, resulting in another uprising. We lost twelve more guards, leaving us with ten for the remaining two hundred people, including my five personal guards. I can't give up my guards because there would be no one left to captain the ship.

After that, we convinced most of the non-infected to come to the Clean Bay without much fuss. We have treated everyone with a new vaccine being evaluated on Earth, which had to be administered by the guards, and we are hopeful that there will be no new cases. The infected are banging on the sealed entryway now. They are calling out for family and friends to come to them, to coax them out, but I have guards constantly posted on that door, guns loaded and ready to fire on command. There are too many for the guards to exterminate now.

I'm still in my executive quarters, secured from all this mess. We are still on course, and I will survive this until we reach Mars.

Only two-hundred-and-eighty days left to go.

February 10th, 2090

I stated in a previous entry that all hell had broken loose, but I had no idea what else would be in store.

Yesterday was indeed the day that all hell broke loose. It only got worse throughout the night. Quite a lot of the ones we had thought were clean were infected. It started with a few of them trying to Kiss some of the Clean people, which escalated into violent attacks. Some had their eyes clawed out; others had their throats bitten out. The few remaining guards didn't hesitate to open fire. The survivors panicked, and with nowhere to go, they rushed the guards, trying to get to the only entrance and exit that the guards had been ordered to block. The remaining outside guards were quickly overwhelmed and are now part of the ranks of the infected. Now, there are armed infected among us!

God help us all.

I have activated the locks on the executive level doors, effectively sealing myself, my five guards inside, and my family here, but I soon found out I was wrong. It was my fault. I overlooked them, and I let them join those bastards! My carelessness caused me to lose my precious family.

Hundreds of the infected are crammed into the tight hallway leading to my quarters. They have all been standing completely still and staring straight at the doors, their mouths drooping in a sloppy grin, and those evil, hungry yellow eyes just staring at the thick layer of glass that separates me from becoming one of them. They have no way of getting in, so they bang on the door occasionally while they all just chant.

"Let... us... in... Captain."

Over and over and over again, in a chorus of hundreds of voices, they repeat it. The words are burrowing into every nerve, down into the marrow of my bones. I don't know how much longer I can take it.

One of my guards looked at me with fear, covering his face in a mask of petrified terror.

"They're coming after you, Captain. Not us, but you. It's you they want."

"They want me because I know how to fly the ship. They want my brain."

"Then, why not give them what they want?" said another guard. "Can't you see that we're doomed? There's no hope!"

They grabbed me by the arms and muscled me out the door while the other three looked on with approval. The chanting stopped. I turned and looked at the crowd outside my door, the sea of yellow eyes staring back at me vacantly. That was when I saw them; my wife and son were among the group, standing at the very front of the crowd.

I screamed and cried. I had somehow been so concerned with my well-being that I failed to notice that my family was not with me, that they were out there in all the chaos. My poor Martin. He had been so disturbed by what happened in Quarter B that he hadn't spoken in days, and my beautiful wife Reyna, with those big blue eyes, was now forever tarnished in that ugly yellow. The guards changed their minds at the last moment after I shook myself free, and they willingly walked through the sealed doors to join the infected. I was baffled and appalled.

I deserve this.

I am now alone.

Earlier, I sent an alert to the people of Mars. I am sending these message logs to let you all know how close you came to destruction and being one of them. As I typed this last message, I changed the ship's course. The ship will fly directly at Earth's Moon and hopefully explode into a million pieces on the gray, monochrome soil.

Let it be known that I did everything to the best of my ability to save humanity. I hope that my sacrifice will be forever remembered.

February 11th, 2090

You have nothing to fear. We are One.

We will not hurt you if you comply with our simple request.

There is no reason to fear us.

What is wrong with never dying, never getting sick, never feeling those annoying human emotions?

We are not separate from you, but we are you. Please think of us as humans... evolved.

It is the next logical step for human evolution.

If you are wondering, it was easy getting in. The captain ruined his last chances of safety. We were able to pry open the door and convert him in seconds. We are heading straight for you again, Mars, with the new and improved Captain at the controls.

You humans and your pesky, selfish need for war. It was your downfall, just like the good Old Captain. The Old Captain was too concerned with himself and failed to notice that we converted his wife and son. Now, I am reunited with my family once again.

Now, do you see how flawed you humans are? When you humans discovered the spore, it was your lust for money and war that we thrived upon. We have yet to find another species of creature that wages war for peace.

We are coming. It is only a matter of time before we land amongst your people, and we will spread like wildfire, we will devour your minds, and we will take what we want the most...

YOU.

I NEVER KNEW THAT I HAD A BROTHER

GROWING UP WITHOUT a father wasn't easy. Mom always had trouble keeping men around. She hopped from one to another regularly because few men can stand raising someone else's kid. Because of that, I taught myself to not get too attached. So, she spent most of my childhood working herself to death while I barely saw her. I almost never went to social functions, and anything extracurricular like Girl Scouts, sports or dances were out of the question until I was old enough to ride the bus or drive.

I remember being very jealous of the other girls who brought their dads to after-school activities and seeing the dads playing with their daughters in public, and I will admit that I felt a tinge of anger whenever I saw it. There were others that had the same problem, but for some reason, I was the favorite target of the bullies. Some girls could be real bitches about it. They would giggle and offer their unwanted perspectives on the subject. Some of them grew up without a father too, but they still liked to make the wound deeper.

Here's a recap of one particular incident:

"Look at Amy! She's so ugly that her dad left when he saw her!"

"Oh please! He left before she was even born because he knew what a fugly kid she would be!"

"Hey, Amy! Have you even met your dad? I doubt he'd want anyth…" that was the last thing she said before my fist met her lips and loosened several of her fucking skanky teeth. It was the most talked about thing in school for about the next week or so. I learned that fighting back only managed to stifle the taunting for a brief period. Bullies seek you out to make themselves feel better by using you as a punching bag for their insecurities. Once the bullies learned that they could get a reaction from you, everyone had to take their shot.

I spent most of my teens in practical isolation. I had few friends that I could trust. My best friend, Maci, was the closest person in my life. For years, I trusted her with my deepest thoughts and buried emotions that I hid from everyone else in the world. My mother was too busy working and trying to find a reliable life partner to make time to focus on me and my problems. Eventually, Maci and I would admit our very real love for each other and became very close partners.

It was Maci that I confided in when I received a strange message on Facebook one afternoon.

"Hello, Amy. You may not know who I am, or even that I exist, but we share the same father. I've never met him myself, and as far as I can tell, you haven't either. I'm sorry that this seems out of nowhere, but I've had to deal with therapists my entire life, and I just need to talk to someone that can relate to my abandonment issues. If you choose not to respond, then I'll respect that, but I would love to talk to my sister."

The guy's name was Chase. My mother had told me that my sperm donor had other children with other women before him, and probably after as well, but I never had intentions of ever finding them, or even trying to. As far as I was concerned, the man never existed and never would.

I hesitated for a few days before I responded. I checked out his Facebook profile first. We had some similar tastes in music and TV shows, which I found odd and that terrified me a little. Another thing that I found odd was how much we looked alike. I was my mother's only child, so the idea of having at least one brother out there, who also resembled me quite a bit, was very strange. Maci suggested that I should respond with something harsh, just in case he was sent by my sperm donor of a father to try and coax me into talking to him.

My response was this:

"Sorry for taking so long to reply back. I've never had anyone from this side of the family contact me, so this is all a bit weird. I've never met the man, as you suspected, so the idea of suddenly having siblings was a bit of a shock. My mother never had any other children, and it took a while before the realization sank in.

All that I can say is that man is scum. He left before I was even born. I'd be happier if you would've told me he was dead, to be frank. Where was he when I was sick? Or when we were kicked out of our apartment because my mom couldn't get enough hours at the restaurant? If you're trying to get me to contact him, please, just don't bother."

It took him a few days to get back to me as well. He read it not even an hour after I sent it. After a day, I concluded that he would never reply and that would simply be the end of it. Then he replied with this:

"Hi again, Little Sister. Sorry. Long night at work. Was a bit busy. I read your message and totally forgot to reply. Anyway, I'd like to have lunch with you one day, or preferably dinner, since I'm used to an overnight schedule. I'm sure you've seen my Facebook profile and know where I live, so just let me know when and where, if you're up to it."

My creepdar went off, all sirens blazing. 'Little Sister' he called me. He didn't fucking know me, never fucking met me. What's up with this dude? What was he aiming for? He had the same last name as my father, and he did look like me, but what was his real goal? For all I knew, he could've been the next Jeffrey Dahmer.

Maci practically begged me not to meet him, but I told her that I wanted to. If he was going to be weird about it, I'd tell him off, make a scene, and block his weird ass. Easy as that, or so I hoped. I wanted to make it somewhere public, where plenty of people and security cameras would be. I told him I wanted to meet at the Chinese restaurant inside the local mall. The lobby has lots of cameras pointed towards the seating area, so it seemed safe enough.

"Calm down, Maci. You can come with me if it'll make you feel better," I told her as we watched a show on Netflix that I wasn't paying attention to.

"Yes, it would! I'll make it not obvious. Like I'll come up the escalator while you two are eating and be like 'Oh, Amy! Didn't expect you here!' or I can get a table nearby. I just want to make sure you're safe, babe."

I laughed, "Yeah, sure. Whatever floats your boat, lady."

I met him the following Saturday a few minutes past 6pm, three hours before the mall closed. He was taller than I expected, and a little on the chubby side. He wore a faded shirt of a metal band that I knew of, and a few easily recognizable tattoos on his arms. In any other circumstance, I'd classify this guy as a douche and do my best to not speak to him. He saw me and started waving his arm in the air like a doofus.

"Amy! It's good to meet you finally!" he said, with arms open for a hug.

"Hi, Chase," I replied, with no hug.

"You're shorter than I imagined. Is your mom short too?" Well, he already pissed me off, "Don't talk about my mom."

"Chill. I was just kidding. Gees. You're about as warm as a block of ice." This was when I caught him leering at me. Just for a second or two, but it was definitely a creepy way of checking me out.

"That's me. Thanks for the astute observation, pal," I said as I pulled up a chair. "Now, tell me why I'm here. Really. What do you want?"

"I just want to get to know my sister."

"Cut it. I'm not your sister. We just happen to have the same guy as a father. He was never around either of us. We have never known each other, never met. I'm twenty-nine now. What makes you think I want to know anything about his pathetic life?"

"Well, I see that his absence has made you a tough person, but I'm not like him. I've never been married because I can't trust anyone, no children either because I'm afraid of becoming like him. I drank my youth away, and here I am, thirty-five, and I still work a bullshit job. So, can you be nice before I just leave?"

I stood up, almost knocking the chair over, "No. Me first." I turned and left, almost running face first into Maci, who had just come off the escalator to the food court. She mumbled something as I grabbed her by the sleeve and pulled her along with me.

"That bad?" she asked as we headed back down the escalator.

"That dude gives off hardcore creeper vibes. I'm not sticking around."

"Why?"

"I caught him staring at my tits. What brother does that to their sister?"

"Ew! Yeah, good point."

I wanted to leave, but Maci talked me into walking around the mall for a while to cool my temper off. We walked from store to store, mostly browsing but not buying. She was making fun of people from a distance, trying to make me laugh. My mind had finally moved past the weird man who claimed to be my brother. Maci and I walked toward the parking garage when I told her that I had to pee and that I would be out in a few minutes. I was almost in the women's bathroom near the entrance of the mall when I felt a sharp blow to the back of my head.

I woke up some time later in a haze of blurry pain. I remember my head lolling toward the floor, the haze of unconsciousness slowly fading away. I was in an unfinished basement—the walls were all bare cement blocks, the skeleton of a wooden frame in the ceiling, the floor was bare dirt. A few feet in front of me was a large, shoddily built table. On the table lay multiple tools, most I recognized as tools to butcher meat. The basement was really dark, except for a little moonlight shining in through the tiny windows near the ceiling. I fidgeted but could not budge the binds around my wrists and ankles.

"Well, hello, sister! I'm glad to see you awake! I was beginning to worry about you!" I heard the voice of my 'brother,' but I could only see the outline of him.

"Why did you do this? What do you want?"

"What do I want? That's a funny question. I mean, isn't that obvious?" he answered, stifling a hearty laugh. He put his hand on one of the tools that was on the table. It was a meat cleaver. But I noticed something odd. His hands weren't the same; they were clawed, and the skin was snake-like.

"Relax, sister. It'll all be over soon. I promise." He took a few steps forward, and I could see his face. Protruding from his mouth was this thick, forked tongue from between rows of pointed, barbed teeth. He stepped forward into the light a little more, and I noticed his bulbous black eyes staring at me. His skin had turned thin and scaley with various shades of green.

Panic set in when my brain refused to accept that this was possible. All my animal instincts kicked in to get the fuck out of there. I wiggled with all the strength I could muster, but the ropes were tightly wound. I groaned in pain but kept trying.

"Good luck, little sister. You won't break yourself free. My mother taught me well." He laughed at his own revelation. "You said you didn't want to know about Father, right? Well, I suppose it's time you know what really happened to him. Why do you think he never came back, Amy? Because he made love to my mother who, in turn, devoured him afterward!" he was laughing in an awful, raspy way that barely sounded human. It made my skin crawl to the core.

He stepped forward into the light. His green skin flexed under his worn metal band shirt as he lifted the cleaver. From behind him, a voice exclaimed, "Amy! Are you down there?" I thought I recognized the voice, but my throbbing head made it impossible to analyze that.

My brother's head shot around in the direction of the basement stairs. I heard footsteps rushing down the stairs with the shape of a person. A struggle ensued. I heard a woman grunting and swearing, and my brother growling inhuman sounds, when suddenly, he exclaimed loudly as his body collapsed. From behind him appeared the other shape, who quickly jumped over his body and ran toward me. It was Maci.

"Amy! Oh my God! It took me forever to find you!"

"How did you…?"

"You left you GPS on your phone, thank God. I used an app to find you. His neighbors probably think I'm the biggest creep ever, but it only said you were in a fifty-foot radius of this place. I peeped down through one of those windows up there and saw you," she explained as she cut through the ropes with a knife off the table. "He left the backdoor open, so I went in. I had to save you, babe." She was breathing heavily and was trying to catch her breath. "Is that the creep from the mall?"

"Believe it not, but it is," I said as she helped me off the table he tied me to.

As soon as I stepped down, I felt a horrific pain in my left leg. "Oh, God! Something hurts, Maci. Oh God! My left leg!" She stopped and helped me sit down on the table. I looked down and saw my brother laying on the ground, a growing pool of black blood circling his body. He wasn't about to get up.

"Oh my God, Amy! He tried to eat your leg!" I looked down and saw a massive chunk of my thigh was gone. The white of the bone reflecting in the dim moonlight. I suppose it's not too surprising that I fainted then. Maci said she carried—partially dragged— me to her car and floored it to the hospital. She told the staff that I had texted her and she found me this way. It was a few days before I came out of it.

They said they tested me for a variety of diseases, and all came back negative, so that's a major plus. It has been a little over a week and I've had a lot of time to think about it. I think that I can make peace with my father now. All the sadness and heartache I felt as a kid now just seems null and void. In place of those emotions, I feel appreciative of what I did have, for all that Mom did for us, instead of focusing on what I didn't have. I also feel sad for my father. Who knows what it must've been like to be eaten by one of those creatures?

While I was in this hospital, I dreamed about my brother, dreamed about his barbed teeth digging into my flesh, tearing, and pulling chunks to feed his endless hunger for human meat. Each time, it became more and more vivid. They continued even after we came back home, and three nights ago, the dreams changed. He was ripping apart Maci and invited me to join him. Eventually, I accepted.

The next morning, I woke up on the floor, drenched in blood. It took some time for my brain to comprehend what it was. How it got there, I wasn't sure. I rushed into the shower a couple rooms over from me, taking the equivalent of at least ten normal showers, but I never did feel clean. I made my way back to our bedroom and found Maci sleeping comfortably.

I swear, I don't remember doing it. I have zero memory of killing someone or something. Then yesterday, I started having this insatiable craving. This powerful hunger for meat. I walked to the kitchen and ate an entire pound of raw hamburger, but that only curbed the craving. I remember looking down at my leg that night and the flesh had grown back, along with green reptile-like skin. By the next morning, it had spread across most of the lower half of my body. I contracted something from him, some disease that is slowly transforming me into the monster that he was.

And so, yesterday evening, I finally did it. All that I can remember was hiding behind some bushes for a woman jogging by. I pulled her into the bushes and ripped out her throat with my teeth. The blood felt as good as I imagined, and I felt this beast inside of me awaken, craving more, so I continued eating and drinking in the red liquid of life as it poured into my mouth. Her body flopped around in my grasp, but I held on with strength I didn't know that I had. She gurgled as she choked to death on her blood and that only intensified the satisfaction. That feeling, oh that feeling, it was better than sex, better than any orgasm.

Once I was full, I realized that if anyone came in, I'd be done for. I dragged her body to a house currently under construction, shoving the remains of her body through a basement window. I fell into the bushes beside the hospital and ran like hell into a nearby alleyway. I remember running down to a nearby river, ditching my clothes and bathing off as much of the blood and carnage as I could, and ran the rest of the way home completely naked. Thankfully, I didn't see anyone else.

Here I am, at home now. I took another long, warm shower once I woke up and remembered what happened, and I slept the best sleep of my life. Before I finally cease to exist as a normal human being, I wanted to put my story out there, as a warning. Be very, very wary of disassociated family reaching out to you on the internet.

THERE'S SOMETHING INSIDE OF ME

I WAS ONCE AN ORDINARY man. My life was mundane and uneventful, and honestly, I loved it being that way. Parties and socializing terrified me. I've always been afraid to be in a large group of people, and I am awkward to the point of it being painful. What I mean is that I become overstimulated, which births a panic attack, and eventually, I vomit whatever I've eaten at said event, which is rather embarrassing.

Being alone suited me just fine.

Believe it or not, I've been able to maintain relationships with the opposite sex. I've had several serious girlfriends, but none lasted six months. Eventually, they tire of staying home with me and watching movies or TV shows. They will want to hang out with their friends and show me off to them like some prized show dog, and then their friends are weirded out at how I stand around, barely speaking. The woman will find some way to call it quits and move on to someone more suited to their social needs.

That is, until I met Emma.

Emma and I have been together for seven years now and married for five of them. We've created a relationship that neither of us thought achievable, but both sought after in our dreams. She is like me—she hates socializing, loves watching horror movies and TV shows, and has no desire to be anywhere without me.

It's wonderful.

One night, I was awakened from sleep by the sudden horror of suffocation. I bolted upright in bed, clutching at my throat.

Something was stuck in my throat. And it was crawling.

I could feel its little feet slowly clawing individually down the fleshy tube. Each little movement felt like a tiny needle digging into me from the inside. I managed to wake Emma by slapping her in panic.

"What's going on?" she said sleepily. It took a few moments for her brain to register that this was real and not some lucid nightmare.

She screamed, "Oh my God! Paul!" as she wrapped her arms around my midsection and began to perform a very rough version of the Heimlich Maneuver.

One. Two. Three.

Instead of popping out of my mouth, whatever the thing was fell into my stomach. I could feel the thing plop into the space and burrow itself into my stomach wall. I'm not sure how to describe what that felt like, but the pain was enough to make me double over in jaw-clenching agony.

But strangely, once the thing was done, I no longer felt pain. "Paul, are you all right?" she asked me repeatedly in her motherly way. I love how much she cares about me and always makes sure that I am okay.

We both concluded that it must've been the Chinese takeout we had for dinner, that maybe I had vomited some of it up into my throat, where it became lodged and caused that bit of traumatic hell. Emma handled it with the tenderness of a sweet, loving angel, making me feel completely safe and secure. About an hour later, I drifted back to sleep peacefully.

The next day, I felt fine and decided to go to work. While at work, I can fake my way through any social situation with an occasional "Wow!" or "That's crazy!" and maybe even add a smile or nod for good measure. Most of the day, though, I am in my little cubicle by my lonesome. I answer my tickets promptly and call when needed; otherwise, the ship stays afloat without me needing to leave my pod.

As lunch approached, I found the hunger pains more intense than usual. That morning, I stopped at a convenience store to refuel the car and bought a breakfast sandwich and one of those pre-made bottled iced coffees that are way overpriced. I usually don't, but after the episode the night before that caused a lack of sleep, I needed *something* to kick me into gear. The clerk, an awkward-looking brunette girl I probably would've fancied in my younger years, was nice enough to warm up the sandwich. That hadn't been enough to satiate my stomach.

An hour before lunch, I was beginning to get sick hungry; that feeling where you might pass out if you don't eat something soon. I dug through my desk, but I found no snacks. For lunch, I was going to walk across the street to the sub restaurant to pick up the order I had placed on my phone. I also scoured through my desk for any loose change because our vending machines had yet to be upgraded to take cards, and they accepted cash only like this was 1999.

That was when I found something.

It was a pencil I kept stashed away when I had to write something on a Post-It Note. My growling stomach told my brain, "Eat it."

And so I did, without any hesitation.

I chomped into the wood like it was a damn chocolate bar, and holy crap, did it *feel* like I was eating one. My brain broke into that same endorphin rush that only the best candy bars can induce. Splinters of wood stabbed into my gums and the roof of my mouth, but it didn't hurt. No, I would say the sensation was nearly orgasmic. I chewed and chewed until the wood was down to the little metal nib where the eraser was, which I discovered is called the ferrule. I hastily removed the little pink chunk of rubber and popped it into my mouth like a gumball.

I'm just thankful nobody walked by my cubicle while this was happening.

It didn't stop there.

When I made it home, Emma had gone to the grocery store. I searched around the refrigerator, the cabinets, and the dry goods cupboard but found nothing appetizing. My mouth was dry, my stomach an earthquake of growling and tightness.

That was when I locked eyes on the kitchen sponge.

It was still moist from Emma cleaning the dishes earlier that day. I picked it up and inhaled the scent of the menagerie of old food, crust, and probably bacteria it had wiped away during its lifetime. The odors drove my taste buds mad. I *had* to take a bite.

My teeth sank into the juicy polyurethane, and my mouth flooded with dirty water. The sensors in my brain reacted as if I had just taken a large gulp of an ice-cold soda on a hot day. I ripped a chunk off the sponge the same way one would do with a thick steak. I chewed the piece, wringing every drop of moisture from it before I swallowed it. I did this repeatedly until the last piece entered my increasingly content stomach.

With that, my appetite would go back to normal.

This went on for over two weeks. I would eat whatever my stomach suddenly decided it wanted to. From crayons to various paper products to a urinal cake, I glanced at it in the office restroom.

Until the cravings began to change.

On my way to work one morning, I was driving around a sharp curve when I noticed a dead squirrel lying on the road. My front right tire nearly hit it, but I was careful not to. I had plans for the deceased critter. Its death must've been painless because once I pulled over and got out to examine it, I discovered its head was nothing but a mushy puddle on the road. I walked over to the carcass, and the cravings kicked in again.

I squatted down to examine the poor creature and to say a short prayer, but then the smell of its blood and brains wafted up my nose, activating something in me. I saw a car coming in the other direction, so I scooped up the remains, wrapped them tightly in a plastic bag, and tucked them into my lunch box. By the time I had done this, the car had passed me moments before. I squatted down again at the spot where it died.

I had to admit it, but I licked it. I licked the asphalt slowly but eagerly, like a child with a delicious lollypop. Bits of fur and bodily matter caked the inside of my mouth, but it was the blood I was craving. Another car came around the bend, forcing me to stop and jump back into my car. I wiped my mouth with napkins from a fast food joint and chugged coffee to get the smell off my breath. When that didn't work, I ate a handful of breath mints I had learned to keep handy when those urges hit.

At lunch that day, I hid in the bathroom with my newly found prize. It felt like Christmas Day as I unwrapped the precious little gift. My normal mind took a backseat as I devoured the little corpse with the voracity of a starving wolf. Once I had eaten every piece of meat from the creature, I flushed the remains down the toilet and then washed off the aftermath in the sink.

About thirty minutes later, someone walked by my cube while chatting with someone.

"It smelled like a friggin' corpse in there. Whoever did that needs to see a doctor ASAP."

I had to cover my mouth to stifle the laugh that came out of me. I couldn't stop myself. This horrible new habit I had to hide from everyone made me insane. It was a tremendous effort to keep this from Emma. I couldn't let her find out, even if that meant lying to her. Having her even want to be around me was a miracle in and of itself, and if she found out about my dirty secret, I was afraid she'd leave me for sure.

Looking back, I don't think I laughed because I thought it was funny—I was laughing because I was terrified. It only continued to get worse from there.

Roadkill satisfied those cravings for a time. The only ones that seemed to quench it for the longest time were the fresh ones that still had some blood left. I found myself intentionally swerving or speeding up to hit a rabbit, a snake, or even a bird if I had the chance. Birds are much more difficult to hit intentionally. I killed more in my driving history unintentionally than I ever did on purpose. The cravings were turning me into a feral beast, hellbent on doing anything possible to achieve satisfaction. I wondered if this is how junkies feel, the insatiable urge to curb the desire no matter the cost.

During this stage, there were a few times that Emma nearly caught me. I had been eating a dead possum off and on for an entire Saturday, hiding it inside the toilet tank in a plastic tub. I realized I hadn't thought of a way to dispose of it without her knowing. I tried to sneak outside, but she was stationary on the couch by the front door, reading a new book. I couldn't dump it out the window because then there'd be questions about who left the animal carcass, and it could point back to me. In a panic, I decided to try to flush the bones. Luckily, the head had been obliterated by traffic, so all that I had to flush were the smaller bones. At least, I thought that was going to be easy enough.

The toilet began to back up and flood the bathroom.

I began to yell obscenities and desperately tried to plunge the remains back down, but nothing was working. Emma heard the commotion and came in.

"What's going on?"

"The damn toilet backed up."

"Oh God, Paul. It smells like a corpse in here. What did you eat?"

"It wasn't me. I think something got into the pipes and died."

She did her best to help, but we were unsuccessful. When she proposed calling the landlord, I relented. They called a plumber, who was at our apartment within a few hours.

"I'll be damned. Not the first time I've seen this, but it's not very common. Looks like ya got a dead rat, a raccoon, or sumtin' that got into the sewer pipes and drowned. Looks like it a big bastard, too." The plumber told us, laughing at his observation.

No kidding, I thought.

The carpet had to be replaced, but the wood underneath appeared okay, according to the landlord. They were nice enough not to charge us anything for the 'accident.' Emma never questioned what the plumber concluded, and we continued our lives. I, on the other hand, was turning into something that could've only existed in my nightmares before the choking incident. The cravings turned from occasionally running things over to me actively looking for small animals to kill.

One evening, after I had to work overtime to fix a significant system-wide problem, I stumbled across the annoying orange cat that we nicknamed Fatty. Fatty was a very well-fed cat that had a habit of climbing onto the cars in the parking lot and leaving his little paw prints as evidence. His little paw prints can also scratch your paint with his little claws. That evening, Fatty jumped onto my hood as soon as I parked.

Already annoyed at the day, I jumped out to shoo him away, but instead, he plopped his fat behind down and just stared at me. He was definitely taunting me.

Ha-Ha. You idiot. I run this place, and you happen to live in it. Go away so I can ruin the paint on your car with my tiny claws.

I yanked Fatty by the scruff and was met with swinging claws and growling. I remembered that I had forgotten to leave my box cutter at work. After retrieving the box cutter from my pants pocket, I dispatched the troublesome Fatty.

That wasn't all.

Once I smelled the blood, the cravings intensified. I lapped the pouring blood from Fatty's neck, much like a cat would drink water. Oh, it was glorious. I felt satisfied that Fatty would no longer mess up our vehicles, but I was also relieved by my feeding. I retrieved a plastic bag, which I always kept handy lately, rolled up Fatty nice and tight, and then hid him in my lunchbox.

I ate him for a late-night snack and lunch the following day. The odd snacking still occurs. Sometimes, I'll drink liquid paper, eat the stuffing from chairs, and even drink glass cleaner. I'll never know how this stuff hasn't killed me. Whatever triggers my hunger, I can't say no; I physically can't stop myself. It had become a full-blown addiction.

I was tracking down a stray dog when a homeless man grabbed me by the sleeve.

"Hey, mister. Ya got five bucks to spare?"

His breath had the rank smell of cheap vodka and tooth decay. He didn't appear to have bathed in months, maybe even years. The poor fellow didn't expect me to pounce on him and tear at his jugular with my teeth. He was the first.

Things have not been so simple since that started. Sure, I still get the urge to consume manufactured products and the occasional roadkill, but when the craving for meat hits, I try to stay away from other people. I do everything I can to do it. The only thing else I could think to do was fully restrain myself, which is where I'm going with this.

The last and final straw hit me last night. Emma and I were watching one of our favorite paranormal shows when we decided it was time for bed. We made love and just laid there in the bliss of it. I rolled over and noticed that she had a scab on her leg from shaving. I picked at it, and she winced.

"Careful. I finally decided to shave my Sasquatch legs. Did you notice?"

"N-no. Just did."

"Are you okay?"

She noticed that I was trembling. My muscles began to tighten, and sweat began to flow from every pore. I excused myself and went to the bathroom. She knocked on the door to check on me again, and I told her I was okay. I came out thirty minutes later, and she was asleep. Thank God. Thank whatever God is up there that I could get out of there.

I went into the kitchen and ate an entire pack of raw hamburger meat to at least drive down the intensity. I began to cry after sneaking out the front door and down to my car.

"No! No! Please, God! Not her! Anyone but her! I can't! I just can't!"

I started thinking about ways to end my life. I concluded it was the only way to stop this unbearable condition once and for all. I don't own a gun, but I have several large knives that I have collected since I was a teenager, but that sounded like it would be too traumatic. What if Emma found me like that? I couldn't just leave her. I waited for her my entire life, and I'd leave her in such a cowardly act? I knew from my experiences that pills or other chemicals would probably not affect me in the same way as an ordinary person. What else could I do?

I thought of one other way. I'm turning myself in.

Over the last two years, I've killed and partially consumed fourteen people across three neighboring states. Emma will not be one of them. I can't hide this anymore; she will not become another victim of this never-ending madness. I don't know how I've managed to keep this up for this long. I suppose the desire not to lose her kept me going.

Emma, if you're reading or listening to this, I hope you know how much I love you.

There's something inside of me that I can't stop or control, and I don't believe I can ever truly be rid of it. If I catch a certain smell of you, I don't know if I can escape before it takes hold.

I can't risk it.

I hope you find happiness again, and I hope you find someone better. This wasn't your fault. This was that thing that crawled into my mouth that fateful night.

I hope you find someone who doesn't turn into a cannibalistic monster.

SCRATCHES

I'M JUST A TYPICAL GUY. I don't consider myself crazy, but then again, crazy people don't think they are. Maybe I am, then. I used to spend much time at home playing games, pretending to be the hero I wasn't. Little did I know that some of that would come in handy. We had four cats, and there was usually a cat wherever you would go, even when I went to the bathroom; the one place you go for privacy and a damn cat would want in to rub on you and climb into your pants.

Scratch.

Scratch.

Scratch.

It never failed.

One night, I was doing my business and heard the scratches. Instinct kicked in and started calling out for them to leave.

"Go away!" I said, "Fucking cats…"

It continued. That was when I noticed something different this time. Something didn't sound right. The scratches sounded deeper, harder. Not what a cat should be capable of. I paused, listening to the wood being dug off my door, and then it stopped. I had my phone in my hand, and my brain told me to contact my girlfriend, but then I remembered she was at work.

Shit.

The scratches started a few seconds later, and then it called out to me.

"Eric." It was more like a whisper, but sounded harsh and raspy, not quite human.

My blood started pumping, and the adrenaline kicked in as panic started its rampage through my body. I have high anxiety but fuck, that certainly didn't help. Sweat popped up on my brow while my brain tried to comprehend what was happening.

Did I lock the door? Did someone come in through a window? Did they break in, and I was too distracted reading dumb shit to hear it?

A little hand poked under the door. It was bigger than a cat's paw and looked like a sickly human hand with long, sharp—nailed fingers. The hand swung around, searching for something to grab, and retreated under the door. Giggling followed soon after.

"You'll have to come out soon, Eric."

My cats. My poor cats.

They were out there alone. Cats have claws and can defend themselves, but could they fend off this thing? Judging by its hand size, it was an easy assumption I could take on. In the bathroom, I could only fend it off with a can of air freshener. Armed with my mighty can of Hawaiian-scented aerosol spray, I rushed out the door.

Nothing was there. No spindly, humanoid creature like I had pictured. Not even a cat. We lived in a townhouse, and the bathroom was on the top section overlooking the stairs. I looked in the bedrooms, and there was no sign of life. The linen closet in the hallway was empty, too. I was slightly confused, but more alarms went off when it became increasingly apparent that none of my cats were up there lazing on the beds or floors.

I checked around the house and found no sign of a break-in or disturbance. It was odd, but I chalked it up to the air vents making a weird noise. The next afternoon, I walked through the parking lot to my car when I bumped into my next-door neighbor.

"Hey, man. Have you seen raccoons or something lately?"

"Not that I'm aware of. What's up, Jeff?" I asked.

"Well, my cats have been running back and forth, growling, and hissing at something by the sliding back door, and whatever it was got into the trash cans. Garbage was everywhere this morning."

"No, I haven't, but I'll watch. Thanks for the warning."

I thought that was odd, considering that Jeff rarely spoke to me. Usually, he would ask if we were also having internet issues.

After turning on the light above the stairs, I saw a trail of blood going down them. The panic intensified, and I was on the verge of an anxiety attack. After getting just beyond the wall on the stairs, I looked down into the living room.

There it was.

I still don't know how to describe it. It was like a little human but with four arachnid-like legs on a thorax. Its body was covered in this black and green shell-like appendage. All four cats were lying dead in various places in the living room, all dead. Their blood had been sprayed on everything. The thing stood there, grinning with its sharp fangs, two much longer than the others.

"Your cats tasted lovely. It's a shame there aren't more." It wasn't whispering that time. For a little creature, it had a deep, intimidating voice.

I freaked out when I saw my dead cats. Two of the four were eviscerated. None of them were breathing. The inner beast in me lashed out. Without a thought, I hosed the little fucker with the can of air freshener. It hissed, growled, and screamed. The thing ran back down the air vent beside the couch where it must've crawled out of. I could hear the sound of it scuttling in retreat through the vent.

That particular air vent hadn't worked in months, now that I think about it, and it's no wonder. I didn't own a gun, so I grabbed a hammer and the biggest kitchen knife we had. After cleaning up my cats' remains, I waited the rest of the night while I thought about how to explain this to my landlord and what to do with my poor cats.

It wasn't easy explaining this to my girlfriend when she came home. Cleaning the mess was a massive feat, but I did my best, given the situation. I put all the cats in boxes that I found and wouldn't let her see them. I taped them shut and kept them out of sight. I told her a raccoon broke in and was the culprit.

I felt terrible for lying to her about it. It took months for both of us to recover. She thought of those cats as our kids and often called them that. It's been a few months, but she seems okay now. She hasn't asked for another cat yet, and I hope she doesn't.

We're moving out soon. She can't handle the memories, and neither can I. I also have difficulty sleeping. Every night, I dream about the scratching and that horrible creature.

FOLLOW THE BLOOD IN THE SNOW

IT WAS A FRIGID AND BITTER December that year. The air was painful and bound to consume you with its biting cold and constant snow. I trudged through ankle-deep snow as more was piling on with every passing moment. I knew my destination was somewhere close by, but it was difficult to see through the blinding rage of the storm. My only guide was the blood in the snow.

I heard it before I saw it. Somebody, or maybe something, was screaming, not very far from me. It was the scream of someone in absolute fear. It was hard to tell which direction it came from, but I ran as far as I could toward where I thought it was coming from.

Before me stood the beast that I had been tracking for days.

For weeks, people in this town had been finding eviscerated corpses, their throats ripped out and large chunks of flesh missing, sometimes with multiple limbs gone. I was hired to handle this problem and wouldn't disappoint them. I had a reputation to maintain.

The beast stood close to seven feet tall. Its large claws hang from its sides in an attack stance. The foam was drooling down its muzzle as its sharp teeth snarled at me in rage. The snow was knee-deep by then and still falling. The winter moonlight was the only thing saving me from destruction. That's when I decided to speak first.

"I know that you understand me. I am doing this for your good."

"I hope… you're ready… to become… supper," it growled back at me.

Between us was a narrow stream of running water that hadn't frozen yet. I raised my pistol, loaded with six silver bullets. The beast lunged, taking one single leap across the eight—feet-wide stream. With one swing from its massive claws, it knocked the pistol from my hand and had me on the ground before I had a chance to fire. My face was bleeding, shredded from its powerful strike. Luckily, the swipe hadn't torn my face off.

"I… told… you… supper," the beast said, laughing at me. It raised its claw that it struck me with, licking away the blood. "Delicious!"

My hat was knocked off, lying a few feet away. I had hidden a silver knife inside the rim, just in case this happened. I leaped toward it, but the wolf pinned my arm down with its foot.

"Fool… you won't…" Bang!

I shot the wolf in its shoulder. The wolf wasn't paying attention when I reached for my pistol. It gave a pained scream of pure misery, running off into the woods. I followed the blood trail for a while, but it stopped at another stream. There were no other signs of where the wolf went.

Back in town, I found the local doctor, who stitched up my wounds.

"They're not as bad as they seem, but you should still take it easy," he tried to lecture me. "Now, I know it's not as bad as it looks, but it needs time to heal."

"I'll be fine. I have no time to rest, unfortunately. Others will die if I rest."

"Well, at least don't let it hit your face again," he laughed. "And try not to shave for a few weeks."

After I left the doctor's home, I went straight to their minuscule town hall, where the town leaders were waiting forme. I informed them that I had shot the wolf, but I hadn't found the body to confirm if it was dead.

"But do you think it may still be alive?" an old man on the town council asked me, very worried and having not slept in a long time.

"It may be still alive, but it may bleed out soon. I would recommend keeping a lookout tonight. It may come back for one last dinner," was my reply. I try to be blunt, but they don't always listen. "It's not a warning; it's a promise. The poison from the silver is running through its veins, and the wolf is most likely going insane from it right now. The silver poison will eat away their brain, similar to rabies but not contagious. It will lash out at anything it sees—men, women, children, or animals. Put guards out tonight; arm them with the silver bullets I gave you when I arrived. This ends tonight!" I said as I shut the door behind me.

They probably won't do a damn thing, I just told them. They're going to expect me to do it all, I thought. I wasn't wrong, either.

One thing that people always get wrong about werewolves is the moon aspect. They are nocturnal, but they don't only show up during a full moon—they're just more active around that time like other animals. It's easier to see, so they'd take advantage of it. Some forms of lycanthropy are worse, but most of the time, they only turn into their wolf form occasionally. It varies, but mostly it's once a week. This one suffers from silver poisoning, so it would still be thrashing through the woods in its wolf state.

I waited with the town guards that night, watching them toss back ale after ale. I could piece together why this town had so many victims. A report came in from the eastern part of town, by the farms on the outskirts, of a possible werewolf sighting. I ran over that way with three inebriated guards, making sure they used the silver bullets I had brought in.

"It took Martha! It ran to the woods over there!" she screamed, pointing sternly at the dark trees down the hill slope in the distance. "Kill it! I don't care, but please bring Martha back alive!"

The guards told her we would do our best, and we ran over there with only torchlight to guide us. The night was overcast so that no moonlight could enlighten our path. The guards were jumpy, leaping off their feet at the sound of a twig snapping.

"Maybe if I sneeze, I could kill one of you," I mocked them. "I've... never... seen a werewolf," one of the younger guards squeaked out.

"Well, you're about to. Pull up your trousers and prepare your bowels."

"Why?"

"Because it's a seven-foot-tall killing machine hungry for you." I turned around and stared him in the face. "It will not hesitate for a moment to tear your throat out and rip your limbs off one by one. It would be best not to think this was a child's field trip. This may very well be the last night of your life."

"Got it," was all that he could mutter.

After a few minutes, we heard more screaming deeper into the wilderness. It sounded like a little girl.

"It came from over here," I screamed, pointing, "Let's go!"

We rushed through underbrush and over tree roots; some of the guards stumbled on the way—clumsy buffoons. One of them didn't get back up. He screamed, along with the sound of his flesh being torn apart. From the dim glow of his torch, I saw the furry outline of the massive body of the wolf. With ease, it tore the man's uniform from his chest and devoured his throat. Bloody gurgling was the last sound that came from him.

The wolf looked at me, its muzzle dripping with the man's blood, and I could swear it smiled.

"Soon… I will… eat you, too," was what it said as it hefted the man's body onto its shoulder and ran into the woods.

"After it!"

The remaining guards and I gave chase, except for the scared young man. He was frozen, and I had no time to satisfy him. He eventually decided to follow, and I watched him walking far behind, shivering, and jumping around with his rifle pointed toward every little sound. It was the last time I saw him alive.

As the snow started falling, we pushed through the brush and the dead trees. It quickly turned into a blizzard, and we had to retire our pursuit. We went back for the young man but never found him. He was gone. When we did see him, it wouldn't be a pretty sight. After making it back to town, the guards returned to their posts, and I waited with a few of them to see if it would turn up again, but it did not that night.

I slept long that night and dreamed about the victims. I dreamed of how each of them was robbed of their lives by this maniacal, endlessly hungry beast and how I wished I could've been here to prevent it. I didn't know these people, never met and never met any of them, but I still feel sympathy for those who die at the hands of something preventable, for those who die due to ignorance or refusal of knowledge, their leaders. I can only do so much because, after all, I am only just another proletariat among millions of others, living in a world overrun with monsters that are both human and inhuman.

The next day, I met with the local leaders, and this time, I gave them an earful.

"Gentleman. I'm sorry, that phrase is too dignified for you all." I threw a pile of papers on their desk. "I have here papers from the local doctor that I obtained before encountering this wolf. Papers show how a young woman named Eliza began developing strange symptoms a few weeks ago. The same Eliza who had disappeared once this wolf suddenly started rampaging around town."

"She was eaten by it! We all know this!"

"No, she was not. I have no evidence that she was taken, and I have not found her corpse," I got up in the face of the older man, accusing me of being a liar, "You are all hiding something, aren't you? What is it? Tell me, or more will die!"

"She… wasn't the first," a short, fat man muttered. "Oh? How long has this been going on?"

"We thought we had it contained," a pathetic-looking bald man holding his hands shamefully in his pockets replied, "We had them killed, and we burned the bodies. We thought that this was going to be over soon."

"We. I keep hearing that word, but who is *we*?"

"All of us on the council."

"Hmm. I see. So, you let a disease spread throughout your town without notifying anyone? Brilliant. How many have died so far?"

"Fifteen," the fat man answered.

"You people and your ridiculous pride. I swear! Round up anyone else who has developed symptoms. I want them quarantined. We may be able to cure them with proper medical treatment," In disgust, I turned to walk away, but I had one more thing to say, "As for all of you, if you develop symptoms, you're going to the burn pile."

It had been fourteen years since the first outbreaks began in the rural areas of England, which then spread to the cities and exploded like a bomb. Hopping from city to city, it became a horrific epidemic. Lycanthropy had taken thousands of victims, and that was when I, and hundreds of others, were hired by the Crown to take care of this mess. They also hired the best scientists in the Kingdom to find a cure. They created a vaccine laced with bits of silver that would chase the disease out in a few days. It would not work if they were in wolf form, so I had to shoot the one that attacked me. It's a shame that it took almost a decade to discover it. We killed thousands, and within a few years, the disease was almost all gone, except for a few pockets across the UK, such as this little shite village.

The following day, we had just finished rounding up the infected at the local church, bringing the vaccine from a neighboring village. The only person that we hadn't confirmed as being dead was Eliza. It was a few nights before she showed herself again.

I was walking with the guards across a bridge over a small stream. I saw her standing on the opposite side, several yards down. I ran through the snow, pistol in hand. Her muzzle was bloodied, but you could see the effects of the silver poisoning in her eyes. The madness had taken over, and her shoulder was necrotic from the first shot. I couldn't miss this time.

She started running at me and was about to leap when I fired. The bullet struck her heart. Eliza fell to her knees, falling onto her back and rolling over.

"I'm sorry, Eliza, my dear. I wish there were another way."

I walked over to her body to make sure she was dead. Her blood was silver. The bullet did its job. I convinced Eliza's family to have her cremated. As for the rest of the infected, they were all cured within a week. Also, thanks to my efforts, the town council members were all rounded up and jailed for their lack of consideration for their people and for breaking several laws regarding the epidemic.

Now, there was a different problem. As I returned to London to turn in my paperwork, a new problem had begun spreading across London.

"How did it begin?" I asked one of my colleagues at the Ministry of Supernatural Affairs.

"We aren't sure, but it began in the slums. Vampirism is spreading like wildfire. We don't know how to handle this."

"Lycanthropy wasn't enough to defeat us, and vampirism won't either."

I was washing my face the following day when I noticed something odd. Two marks had appeared on my neck overnight. "Lovely. It's my turn."

After that, they started coming multiple times a night. I wasn't sleeping at night by then, so I waited for them, taking them down before they got through my window. Outside, it was pure chaos. People were being chased in the streets; the local bobbies initially tried to contain them but gave up. You could see the vampires crawling on the walls like possessed lizards all over the city during the night.

The following morning, I woke up, and my skin had gone ashen gray; my veins looked like rivers in a parched land. My fingernails had also grown substantially, bordering on claws, and so had my incisors. The mirror showed my yellowing, bloodshot eyes. I stared at myself in disbelief, not quite believing what I was about to become.

The office building at the Ministry was empty. Desks had been flipped over, papers were lying about in a chaotic mess, and many bodies of my former coworkers had been completely drained of blood. I checked them, and they showed no signs of turning. I had gone there to find a book in the upstairs library on how to kill vampires. I found it, but the hunger was trying to take me over by then. The resulting migraine was trying to overpower me, but I wouldn't let it.

The book said to cure vampirism truly, you had to kill the Alpha Vampire that started it. No one was sure why that worked, but in all instances, it did. I decided I only had about two days left before I turned as well, so I had to act with great haste. With only myself to work on the case, I wasn't sure how I could do it. Usually, we had an entire Ministry of around one hundred people to scour and gather information, but I was the last one as far as I can tell.

That night, I hid behind a dumpster and waited for one of the bastards to get close. One came scurrying along the wall above my head. It looked down at me, hissed, and leaped onto me. After a few wrestling moments, I broke its arm and pinned its face against the wall.

"Tell me where the Alpha is!" I demanded to know. "Shouldn't you know? You're one of us, idiot!" it hissed back. I mashed its face off the wall again. "Tell me!"

"In the sewers! Under the Ministry of Supernatural Affairs! How did you not notice? You worked there, didn't you?" he said as he eyed the emblem on my shirt. I had forgotten to change during the chaos of the day.

Later, I made my way in from the sewer grate in the basement. There were thousands upon thousands of those beasts down there. I had no chance of getting in by myself. So, I decided on the only choice that I could find logical, given the vastness of the problem. My old suppliers were all gone; they abandoned the city or were turned like the rest. I gathered as much as possible and placed them strategically during the day.

The sunlight started to sting horrifically by then, but I did my best. They also couldn't smell me because I smelled like them by then. It was easy camouflage. It also helped that I had the abnormal strength they all seemed to possess. It only took a few hours to place everything. I planned to cave around the nest and set a massive fire to roar up the sewers and purge them out of the system once and for all. The reason for killing them all is that if I don't, I can at least remove a large portion of their population.

Tonight is the last night of me being any part of a human. By tomorrow, I will be a bloodthirsty beast. I will set off the tons of explosives and barrels of kerosene that I planted along the sewer way tonight. I will kill that bastard, even if I can't do it with my bare hands, but I will do it. I hope that, by tomorrow, I will not be one of them and will become a human once again and continue my assault against the ungodly creations of Satan.

I am writing this to document the events leading up to my contraction of the vampirism disease and before I explode up half of London. I am also writing this to prove that I was not born one and that I am no criminal. If this letter survives, I have succeeded and saved my beloved home country from this terrible plague. Please, don't remember me as a vicious beast of a vampire or as the man who destroyed so much of the city, but remember me for what I was: a human who fought for the survival of our species.

By some miracle, I did survive. Finding this letter in all the rubble that was once my apartment building took me a while. A large chunk of London lay fifty feet below in the former sewers. Yes, I was successful in killing the Alpha Vampire. The rest of his lot perished with him, almost immediately turning into a pile of ashes as they screamed in pain. How did I survive? It was thanks to one of those books I found in the Ministry. It claimed to cure vampirism, but all it did was stifle the advancement of the disease, and I suppose it also stopped me from exploding like the others.

Only a handful of people left after the vampires died off, and we spent months and months cleaning. The Royal Family booked it out of the UK as soon as the outbreak began to look dire, and they returned toward the end of the cleanup. That year, the election cycle was vicious, but things started returning to normal.

The Queen invited immigrants worldwide to move to England, and soon, we became the most diverse country on Earth. I was also knighted for my efforts. She made it a point to pardon my crimes for destroying a large city section because they deemed it necessary to save us all. I also got a nice promotion at the Ministry as the new minister.

When I stated that the "cure" merely stifled the effects, I meant that I still have most of the symptoms of vampirism. I spent many of my early days keeping my fingernails short and having my teeth filed down every few months by a very nice dentist who got a nice tip for keeping his mouth shut. Being immortal also came with it. I haven't aged since the 1890s and try to move occasionally to keep people from noticing. During the 1960s, they shut down the Ministry and incorporated it into the military. Since then, I have been freelancing across the world. During the 1980s, Germany had a somewhat overwhelming werewolf infestation, resulting in East and West Germany uniting to take the problem on together, and coincided with an outbreak of vampirism across Russia, which both resulted in the fall of the Soviet Union. Most of this is kept hush-hush, and all the documents were re-worded for the history books.

I have one more story for you. This story is more recent, so your readers can relate to this one more. As you may know, many odd and weird groups on "Facebook" are dedicated to all forms of life and lifestyles. I was a bit late jumping on this bandwagon, so pardon me for being an older man. I created an account under a false name and frequently crept up certain pages. Young, ignorant vampires like to make these groups where they meet other young vampires for sexual flings, and, on occasion, there are good-sized groups of them creeping into the basement of an abandoned warehouse somewhere. They still don't sense me, so stealth is one of my favorite tactics. Just rush in, light them up with a few hundred rounds of holy water-laced bullets, and then follow up by setting the building on fire.

Sometimes, you will see a new article like:

Horrific Tragedy. Multiple dead were found inside the burned building. Police Suspect Arson.

Or something to that effect. It could very well have been me. Anyway, back to the story.

I was browsing a group on Facebook that went by a name like: "Vampires United; Join Group for Meetups and Hookups!."

Like I said, young and ignorant. A post was at the top of the list of 'most liked.'

Friday, April 8, 2017. Former John's Bar and Grill location on 12th Ave in Charleston, WV. Blood, drugs, and sex! Just flash your fangs at the basement door!

I told you these vermin love basements. At the time, I was about a 7 hour drive from Charleston, and the date was three days away, so I made my way there, checked in to a local hotel, and began scoping the area. It was a stone's throw from the Kanawha River, surrounded by churches and houses, like every other town in this section of the U.S. With ease, I broke into the basement.

You could easily mistake a vampire club for a sex dungeon; mattresses line the floor, drug paraphernalia scattered randomly, and the occasional BDSM equipment. There were still a few things down here from its days as the bar and grill, like the sign hanging on the front of the building, was still down there and had been spray-painted with stupid, childish phrases. I checked around for a good hiding place and found a closet that wasn't being used.

After ensuring the place was still vacant the morning before, I hid in the closet and waited for my opportunity. Once the place was filled, I turned on the gas from the old grill, waited for the place to fill up, and threw in a lit match. The resulting explosion was heard for miles.

I, unfortunately, was also hurt. It's not one of my best plans to date; even wise older men like me make some mistakes.

However, if you need to get rid of some pesky vampires, werewolves are making your town a living hell, or Bigfoot is riding the Loch Ness Monster across your town bay, call me.

I'm always for hire.

ELLIE VS. THE INFECTED

I SAT ON THE ROOF OF MY house as the town that I grew up in, the town that I had loved and had so many memories in, burned to the ground. I watched it all crumble, watched it all be devoured by the hungry flames. They still survived; they were still walking. By they, I mean the infected. Those who came down with the virus that infected the entire world. They stumble around aimlessly, bumping and tripping into objects like someone in a deep sleep and biting anyone, or anything really, that gets within reach.

I have no guilt. It was me who started the fire. There were too many of them to fight off single-handedly anymore. They had begun to pour in from, I'm guessing, Pittsburgh, which is the nearest large city. Thousands had flooded in the last week, and it was too much for me to handle alone. I gathered all the supplies I could before setting the blaze—food, fuel, and anything else I would need. Being alone during the worst plague in the history of humankind is boring, but my books have kept me from going insane.

I remember the news channels discussing it when it became a national risk. They said the first reported cases came from small towns across the U.S.; once it hit the big cities, it exploded into a wildfire, spreading across the world in no time. The symptoms were listed as such: extreme stomach cramps, followed by dizziness, fatigue, vomiting, and diarrhea, then by very high fever, leaking sinus cavities, extreme chest congestion with shallow breathing, and then death. They labeled it as a propagated outbreak, meaning it spread from person to person, and it did very fast.

The news channels told us the CDC was working with the WHO on a cure or even a vaccine, which neither ever came to fruition. The U.S. government shut down two weeks after it was declared a global pandemic, thus following the rest of the world's governments, and that was that. We lost power somewhere after that, and I don't remember when exactly.

I wasn't always alone in my mountainside house after the government fell. There were plenty of others. We had an excellent little fortification going at the local high school. Some of the survivors knew how to operate a forklift and had placed cars in precise locations around the building. After a while, we had a miniature wall built. It looked like a castle from a junk collector's wet dream, but it worked. We had guards stationed on top, some improvised gates in place, and even a catwalk around the top of the school. It could potentially have worked forever if the following hadn't happened.

Plenty of ammo, food, water, etc., were stocked inside the school. Word got out, and a group of wandering assholes found out and decided they wanted in on it. At first, they pretended to be a group of lost wanderers and wanted in. We were dumb enough to let them in. Later that night, they distracted the guards with two women who came in with them. They opened the gate and let in the rest of them, who easily outnumbered us. The ensuing firefight roused the curiosity of the local infected, who came rushing over to investigate.

I shot five of them and stabbed a woman. I had watched women kill our guards at that gate, so there was nobody to defend the open gate. The other gates were soon overwhelmed, and the guards retreated. I escaped the back gate and swam for it in the river as the infected poured inside. I was the only survivor. I have gone back there and taken what remains of the supplies occasionally. I know it seems disrespectful, but I have little choice.

The situation here had become so bad recently that I nearly starved to death. The thousands of infected that poured into the town out of nowhere, slashing and clawing at each other, had caused complete and total chaos in their wake. Buildings had windows broken, random objects had been knocked over—like light poles, signs, and statues—and it was nearly impossible to make your way through the streets.

Usually, I would use the rooftop access points we had created across town, with walkways from one building to the next, eventually leading to the school. Unfortunately, that no longer exists, thanks to the raiders.

There was one truck that the group had outfitted with layers of steel and a roll cage before the raiders sabotaged everything. I now happened to possess it. It also just happened to plow over the infected relatively easily. Out of desperation, I plowed through at least a hundred on my way to the school. Once I jumped out, I cut my way through the infected with my machete. Inside, I made haste to grab what I could in as little time as possible and returned to the truck. One of them got me on the leg as I was climbing back in, taking out a chunk of my calf.

I fear the worst, and I know how it works. It only takes three days before your brain liquifies and you become one of them. It is now day two.

He worked at the hospital, so he became infected early on. It was me who put him down. He was in bed, slowly dying from the fever, and at the time, nobody knew what was going on with the virus. Ben died in that bed, and I left him there for the time being. I went to sleep on the couch, crying a little after dawn.

The most awful gurgling noises came from the bedroom, loud enough to wake me up from downstairs.

Upstairs, I found him shuffling his way around the bedroom. Once he heard me, his eyes shot around to look at me. I'll never forget his eyes, the mad starvation on his face, craving for the taste of my flesh. I ran, desperately trying to find the 9mm we kept for emergencies. I found it in the hall closet. He came shuffling down the hallway, his crazed eyes still locked on me. I shot him between the eyes. His brain and blood splattered on the wall and the ceiling.

After sliding onto the floor, I cried some more. Once I came to my senses, I dragged him outside and buried him next to our recently deceased dog, Shane. I thank God, or whoever is up there, that Shane wasn't alive during all this.

Before I went, before I became one of them, I had to give these bastards a black eye and let the world remember that Ellie Kettering-Bishop didn't go down without a fight. My husband is buried in the backyard, and whoever finds this, please bury me with him.

DO NOT ENTER

AS A CHILD, I LIVED IN this beautiful old cottage house. Trees and rolling hills surrounded it. The forests were thick and teeming with places for me to explore, and the hills were always hiding tasty berries during the spring and summer months.

Many of my days were spent running through the fields of tall grass to a nearby pond, watching wildlife, or fishing with my grandpa.

"Lily, one day, this will all be yours. If you want it, that is," Grandpa would jest.

"Yes, Grandpa! I would love it! I will care for all the animals and all the crops, just like you taught me! I'll be a great farmer, just like you!"

"Good. I love this land, too, Lily. It has done well for this family for generations. We have lived here, grown here, grew food here, and built homes. If I could stay here forever, I would."

The terrible day that my grandpa passed away was cold and bitter, which was the exact opposite of his sunny personality.

The snow was piling high, and the wind was unforgivably wicked. He warned my mother and me to stay inside while he went to the barn to ensure the horses were complacent and fed. My father died when I was a baby, and my grandmother died well before I was born, so it was just us three to fight off whatever came at us over the years.

Grandpa didn't come back at night, and we didn't sleep knowing something had to be wrong. Grandpa was strong and able-bodied for a man his age, so we had no doubt he was in trouble. The storm was too bad for us to risk going out there to find him. The next morning, we had to dig our way to the barn using a coal shovel from the fireplace. Mother found him collapsed just outside the barn doors, face-down in the snow. The doctors told us he had a heart attack and was probably dead before he hit the ground.

I take little relief in knowing that.

It was tough making up for what Grandpa did for us. He was a strong old man who had worked hard in the fields his whole life. He could outwork ten men half his age, mother always said. She knew how to tend to the crops from Grandpa, but she couldn't work nearly as hard as he could. We toiled and worked harder that spring than ever, and the crop yield was fantastic. We made more than enough money to live on from the market for the rest of the year, and we even had plenty of food to spare!

During my summer downtime, I spent much time by the lake fishing in the same places Grandpa referred to as his "honey spots." The fish weren't biting that day, so I gave up and wandered the paths through the hills. I remember the breeze that day felt wonderful, making the tall grass whip around like it was dancing. I noticed a path deviating from the main path I had never seen before. Across the path hung a sign in red, hand—painted letters that read 'DO NOT ENTER.'

Of course, I ignored that.

After a few minutes' walk, I noticed something wasn't right—dead trees and withered ones replaced the lush and green trees. I passed various trails that I had no idea about as I went on. I had made the mistake of wandering down a few, and soon, I wasn't sure how to get back home. Something inside told me to keep walking.

By the time I reached the end of one path, every single tree was wilted and rotting, and many had fallen over into a heap of rotting undergrowth. They had all appeared to be that way for a long time, perhaps even longer than I had been alive. There was a massive circle of fallen trees, as if bombs had gone off from a war barrage. All of them had fallen pointed outward from the center, and this ancient wooden box sat in the center of one circle. Common sense would tell you to run as far from there as possible, but young people tend to lack that wisdom.

The box was very old. There were these symbols carved into it that I had never seen before. There was also a chain wrapped around it multiple times. More alarms went off in my head.

Something didn't feel right about this box. I started to slowly back off and kept an eye on this weird box the entire time. Once I had walked back so far, my body was overwhelmed with a strange feeling of relaxation, almost like I had been anesthetized. My body felt relaxed enough to collapse on the ground and go to sleep right then and there, like one of those dead trees.

"Lily?" it was the voice of my grandpa. I was shocked to hear him for the first time in months, but relieved. It seemed like an eternity, but I was happy to hear his voice again. I had missed him more than anything else in the world.

"Grandpa? How did you get here?"

"Don't worry about that, Lily. That box you see before you," he said, pointing sternly toward it, "I need it opened."

"Why?"

"It contains something… special. It will make you happy, my Lily. Happier than an infinite supply of candy and toys could ever do. I promise," I noticed then something odd in the voice. It was cracking a little, just enough to notice.

"You promise? That must be special," the voice started to say.

"I never break a promise. You know that," the voice started to shift a little more. Fear started to set in.

"Yes, Grandpa. 'Don't make promises you don't intend to keep,' you always told me."

"Good girl! Can you do this for Grandpa?"

"As long as you promise that everything will be okay."

"Yes. Yes, it will!" that was when the voice changed into something else. It was now a deep and rough voice, almost gravelly. The transition of the voice was like a radio station bleeding over into another station's frequency. "Be a good kid and fetch me the keys. You know where they are."

I snapped, "You're not my grandpa! Get out of my head!" If anyone had been around, they would've thought I was insane, and I'm pretty sure I am.

Without hesitation, I hightailed it out of the circle of trees as fast as my little eleven-year-old legs would take me. I tried my best to remember how I had gotten there, and by the grace of God, I found the correct path. I made it home with only scraping my knees and legs after I had stumbled during my dash out of that place. Behind me, I locked the door.

My mother had gone to town before I had left and was still out, so I was alone. In my head, I heard a thunderous, punctuating thumping sound. It was slow at first, but then the rhythm became faster and faster. After moving my head around in agony, I realized that it was coming from a certain point in my room. The thumping would speed up the closer that I got to the source. Finally, I pinpointed it to a locked drawer in my grandpa's old room.

"Open it and free me," the voice commanded again. "No! Get out of my head!"

"No, I will stay here, and I will torment you until you get the damned key! If you die, then I will move on to your mother and do the same to her. I care little for you!" the voice informed me. "I just want to be free!"

Without much deliberation, I shuffled around my grandpa's room, looking for the key to that drawer. I checked every nook and cranny I could find under his bed and under the mattress. After a time of fruitless searching, the bookshelf caught my attention. With a quick swipe of my hand, I knocked the books on the second shelf to the floor, and an old key toppled to the ground with a hard, bouncing clank.

I held the key for a while and stared at it. There was an odd symbol carved into the bow of the key. It was shaped like a seven-pointed star but with odd grooves around the points.

After a few seconds of trying to analyze it, I gave up and opened the drawer. Inside was another key embedded with multiple tiny jewels and an eye carved into the bow. It was larger and heavier because it was made of iron and clearly was very old.

"Yes! That's it! Now, free me, child!" the voice commanded and was laughing the laugh of a maniacal madman.

After much deliberation, I decided not to pass this curse on to my mother. I knew that my grandpa wouldn't want me to let something bad happen to my mother. The trip seemed longer than the first time, but I returned to the old box. Now the box and the key were producing the dull thud—only it was very fast now.

"Free me! Free me! FREE ME!"

I opened the box against my better judgment. Inside was a large black spherical crystal sitting on a golden frame shaped like the claws of a hawk. There were multi-colored swirls swimming in various paths inside the crystal. They eventually moved together to form a face.

"Did you bring the vial as I commanded?"

"Yes, I did."

"Good! Now, pour the contents on the crystal, and I shall reward you with whatever your heart most desires."

I stood there momentarily, staring at this object of pure evil. "There's one thing that my grandfather was able to teach me when I was a child…"

"Oh, shut up, child! Not now! No one cares about what your dead grandfather said!"

"Never open that damned box."

"What?"

I removed a large, golden crucifix from my pocket—the end sharpened to a very fine point. I found it amongst my grandpa's things, and something told me I needed it. I gripped it with both hands and jabbed the crystal with everything I had in me. The crystal exploded into a cloud of fragments inside the box. I heard a loud, aggravated hissing and growling for a few moments. The box burst into large, purple flames, and I stood by as the remains burned themselves out.

There are many things that I didn't mention about my grandfather and this land. He was the sixth generation to inherit it. Our family had guarded this object for hundreds of years. The story goes that it was used to contain a powerful demon back in the days of the Romans. They couldn't send it to hell and sent it into the crystal instead. If we found the box, we were never to get very close because if we got too close, it would speak to us and not give up until we did what it said or killed ourselves out of insanity.

Grandpa would tell tales of horrible things that happened to our ancestors who found the box and listened to its commands. He said we hid it deep in the woods where it would be difficult to find. He said our ancestors had spoken of burying it, but then we couldn't tell if we were close. Of all the things he mentioned, the most important was never to free it.

Out of all of our lineage, I wasn't the first to think of breaking the crystal. I think that's why Grandpa had the sharpened crucifix. Why didn't he do it? Was he that terrified of it? I supposed I'll never know.

Do I consider myself a hero? No, but I am glad that it is gone now. I still have nightmares about it, and sometimes, I can that underneath the sound of a strong breeze, of running water, and in total silence, swear, that underneath the sound of a strong breeze, of running water, and in total silence, that I can hear the voice calling my name again, telling me that it wants to be free.

THE VANISHING

THE FORCE OF THE WIND was as if Mother Nature was trying to disrupt them—like she was offended by what they were doing. The trees danced like macabre ballet dancers but cuddled under the warm safety of the comforter they packed with them. They made love while the wind blew a horrific, cold gale outside their tent.

The sex was still good. Matt crawled onto Vanessa and started to kiss her neck while he slowly twisted his hips to grind on her through their jeans. She could feel it growing through his pants as he squirmed. Her body warmed from the sensations of his neck kissing. It made her tense and twitch. She bit her lip from the anticipation of what was to come. She pushed him off and took his shirt off, and then he returned the favor.

Vanessa kissed him as she moved her hand into his pants and grabbed his manhood in her grasp. She played with him for as long as she could stand it. The maddening tension was too much, and so she took her jeans off in seconds and had him inside of her just as quickly. He thrust and pushed as her entire body felt it. His manhood was so firm and warm inside her cold body that it felt like sitting next to a campfire. When he came in her, she felt everything let go, and she came herself. Matt fell off her, out of breath and sweaty—she put her head on his chest and started to fall asleep.

A few minutes after midnight, Vanessa was awakened by a loud cracking sound and a bright flash of light. Scared out of her sleep, she shot up, still slightly out of it from her deep slumber. Her ears rang, and she could hear nothing else, not even the rain. She looked around, searching for the light's source, which had dilated her eyes. Straining to see, she noticed that Matt was gone. Startled, she spun around, looking around the tent a few times, but saw no sign of him.

His side of the comforter was undisturbed, like he had just vanished. In her head, she tried to convince herself that he just went outside to pee or something. This thought would not leave her mind, though:

Where did Matt go?

She convinced herself to brace the storm and look outside the tent, thinking the lightning might have struck him, but there was no sign of him. Another tremendous, loud lightning strike came as she crawled under the comforter. It was too dark to see since the thick rain clouds covered the moon, and her phone flashlight did not reveal any recent footprints in the mud. She went inside to crawl under the comforters and wait for him to come back from whatever he was doing.

Then Matt reappeared inside the tent. His body was mangled and bloody—his face was so swollen Vanessa could barely tell that it was him. He also was missing half of his left arm. It looked as if it had been chewed off. Bloody bits of bone and tendons dangled from the wound. His eyes were glazed over in the blank stare of death.

Vanessa shrieked and tried to run out of the tent, but she tripped over Matt's naked body. She slipped and fell face-first into the mud. As fast as she could, she pushed herself up and ran toward their SUV parked several yards away. The wind had started blowing again with vicious ferocity, stopping her from running as fast as she wanted. Years of being on the track team were helping, but the storm had other plans. She fell again, tripping over something on the ground and splashing in the mud again.

As she was pushing herself up, lightning cracked across the sky. In front of her, down the slope in the large, open field, were what appeared to be a hundred dead bodies, all naked, all mutilated, either dead or dying. She could hear moans and groans from the ones who were somehow still alive, but none were moving. Lightning continued cracking, and more and more bodies appeared along with it. Vanessa was both confused and horrified once she realized the correlation and began to run to her left, away from the bodies, but she soon realized there were now bodies there as well.

Lightning cracked again, and she was gone. A few minutes later, Vanessa was just another body in the field. She was still alive, though—her breathing was limited, and her heart was on the verge of stopping. Her breasts had been cut and punctured, many bones had been broken, and she could barely see out of her swollen eyes.

Blood was pouring out of every orifice, and she knew she was dying, but had no idea what happened or that she had even left the campsite. As she was dying, Vanessa heard voices. They were speaking a language she had never heard before, something she had never heard spoken or anything like it. Her brain was too weak to understand any of this, yet she listened.

It would soon be the last act of her life.

She heard what sounded like cackling and two voices shouting something with glee and excitement, but she did not comprehend a word. Their voices sounded like the boom of thunder and the fierce crack of lightning. All of this would have terrified her had her body not been in the last moments of life. High above, between the flashes and booms, she saw something just through the clouds—a round, silvery disc encircled with beautiful, multi-colored lights.

She listened to their conversation as she was dying—nude, bloody, and cold, in the middle of the field where she and her fiancée had wanted to go camping. It was supposed to be a nice, calm summer evening. It wasn't supposed to be like this. Nothing in her wildest, worst nightmare could have ever prepared her for this. Her body was becoming very weak and limber, unable even to twitch. There was no help, not even a glimmer of hope for her. So, she lay there, and she listened.

Lightning flashed once more, and the craft was now gone. Another flash and the hundreds of bodies in the field were gone as well. Not a trace remained of the events from that night.

Across the country, people were calling in reports of strange objects in the sky, but no one believed them. Hundreds of police reports were filed worldwide, but they were never solved. No one ever made the connection, and these disappearances continued daily. All the world's governments knew, and still do, yet they don't want to scare the public into a frenzy with the truth.

Watch out if you see a storm coming and you catch a glimpse of lightning in the distance.

They might be coming for you too.

MRS. KRAUS S CATS

AS MY THERAPIST, I HOPE you promise to keep your confidentiality agreement. You wanted me to write this because finding the words in person is difficult. This story has never been told to anyone outside the group involved. Please, don't give this to the police; twenty-one years of guilt is enough of a punishment, almost more than I can handle. So, here it goes.

It was the mid-nineties, and being a kid then was much different from being one now. Back then, we spent more time outside and less time playing video games, but not nearly as much as kids do now. Teachers could get by with a lot more, such as their methods of punishment. It was 1995, and I was in the second grade. Our teacher was this bitter old bitch named Mrs. Kraus. She was born in East Germany and was used to living a tough life toiling away for the Communists and getting nothing in return, according to her. She was stricter than most teachers and would punish us for the slightest wrongdoings.

During class one day, my friend Kevin beamed our friend Jordan in the back of his head with a wad of paper, and she took away Kevin's recess for an entire month. A month! From that day, she was our worst enemy.

It started with pranks. First, it was gluing her coffee mug to the desk. Shawn had the idea of unscrewing the bolts on her chair, which consequently caused a hospital visit, and she was out of class for a few days after her head banged into the bricked wall and knocked her out. No big deal, right? It's just kid's pranks and nothing serious. The injury from her chair made us slightly more cautious, and we held off on the pranks for a while.

The next event was around October that year, not far from Halloween. We had a new kid show up. They had just moved to town, and they didn't know anyone. His name was Lester, and he moved here because his parents were divorcing, and his mom found a new job nearby. He was a short kid and had an awkward way about him.

"Mein kinders, this is young Lester Keyes. He just moved here from Pennsylvania. Please, be kind and make this young man feel welcomed in his new town," Mrs. Kraus introduced him as she stared a hole through my friends and me.

It wasn't long before Lester blended in with us. Once he warmed up to us, he showed us that he was braver than we were by a long shot. That kid had no fear, none. Once, we were walking by the train tracks, tossing rocks, and talking about video games. In the distance, a train was blaring its horn as it neared a crossing. He dared us to play chicken with the train by jumping onto one of the ladders while its chugging slowed to adjust for a sharp turn. They didn't go particularly fast in this area from all the curves, but it wasn't the safest to try. None of us would.

"You guys are such chickens! I don't know why I even hang with you!" he started making clucking noises and doing his best chicken impersonation. Still, none of us moved.

"Fine! I'll show you how it's done!"

When the train came, Lester waited a little while as the conductor went around a corner and out of sight. He reared back, and to our amazement, he jumped. We watched as he leaped toward the train, grabbed onto a ladder, pulled himself up, and waved at us as he paraded himself on the ladder like he had done this a thousand times before. I started screaming at him to jump off before he was hurt. It sounded like no matter what I told him to do, he should've been hurt, but he didn't.

Lester jumped down, spiraled mid-air, and landed on his feet like a cat. It took a few moments to get to him, but he laughed when we arrived.

Lester pretended to be fearless, but we found out he had one fear, something that made him damn near animalistic: dogs. We were walking home one evening, right before dusk. We were supposed to be home before sunset, and it was close by then. We walked past Larry Wiseman's house, and his medium-sized mutt approached the fence. It wasn't barking or growling but panting and wagging its tail, waiting to be petted like we had done a hundred times before. Lester saw the dog and seized up; his green eyes grew huge, and he screamed like he was in horrible pain and fled down the street we were going down. It was odd, but we concluded he had a phobia of dogs. None of us had pets, so it didn't complicate our friendship.

Around April of that year, thanks to Lester, we had all become experts in getting away with practically any prank we could dream up. That kid was crafty and was an expert at lying. I thought that was a bit concerning, but as far as I could tell, he hadn't lied to me about anything.

In April, Lester found trouble that he couldn't escape for the first and last time. He was taping an air horn to Mrs. Kraus's chair when she made an expected early arrival back to her classroom from her lunch break. Lester spent the next month in detention instead of recess, and consequently, recess was much more boring. Before that, kids applauded him, calling him The King of Pranks because he was never caught. Mrs. Kraus didn't seem a bit reluctant to punish Lester. Looking back, she must've suspected it was him, but never saw him do it.

Lester barely said a word the next month. He seemed lost in his mind, dwelling on something. When he finally spoke, we were terrified of what he said.

"I want to kill Mrs. Kraus," he said calmly, as if he had just proposed we go explore the creek or go hiking instead.

"What? Seriously?" Kevin spoke first after a few moments of silence.

I was still processing what he had said. Surely, he wasn't serious. There's no way any of us would do it. I don't remember how the conversation went because it's all a blur now. It's the only part of the events I don't remember. All that I can recall is Lester saying, "Don't worry. We won't get caught. I promise," all with a smile, the biggest, toothy smile I would ever see on his face.

The next thing to happen was a few nights before the final events occurred. It had been raining for days. The creeks were overflowing, and my mom said it wouldn't take much for a bad flood, so we may need to evacuate. Later at school, we didn't go outside for recess that day. That was where Lester hatched his villainous plan.

It was close to sunset. We had been hiding behind Mrs. Kraus's house in the woods, stalking her movements for hours. I was so nervous that I was sick, but I couldn't let my friends know that—they'd never let me live it down. Mrs. Kraus had been in her garage for quite some time, toiling around and cleaning things. She kept the door wide open to make it easier to dispose of things. I was surprised when Lester looked at us and waved his hand forward, which was the signal.

He walked into the garage, gasping for air. "Lester? What is the matter?"

"They're.... they're chasing me!"

"Who is chasing you, child?"

I saw Lester look up at the backdoor of the garage, probably looking to see if it was unlocked. After he and Mrs. Kraus went inside, he left the door cracked just enough for us to get in unnoticed. Kevin and I carefully made our way inside. Lester had acquired a large pipe wrench from her garage when he opened the door. You know, the ones painted red that you see every plumber with.

Lester waited for Mrs. Kraus to turn around while I think she was going to retrieve something, and then we heard a meaty *bam*!

Bam!

Bam!

She was down on the ground. The back of her head was completely caved in, brains, hair, and blood splattered everywhere, especially on Lester. That was when Jordan started crying. He was our lookout, but he had decided to peep into the garage and watch what we were doing. Jordan tried to take off running, but Lester tackled him before he made it to the street. He climbed on top of Jordan in the grass and started choking him.

"You little prick! You better not tell anyone… or you're next! You got me?"

"Okay!" was all Jordan could get out through all the airless gurgling. Kevin and I watched helplessly as Lester did so. I had a feeling that if I interfered, it would have ended badly, and I'm assuming now that Kevin did, too.

Lester had Jordan, and I go to the woods and prepare to bury her in the shallow grave we had dug earlier. The ground that day was muddy from the days of rain, but still firm enough not to collapse in on us. By the time we had the shovels and large stones ready, Lester and Kevin had dragged her body up to the grave.

We shoved her in, threw the heavy stones on her to keep animals from digging her up, and threw all the evidence into the rampaging, flooded river. Kevin and Jordan cleaned and bleached the floor of Mrs. Kraus's garage. We had told our parents that we were staying at Lester's house that night, and none of our parents knew that we were out so late.

Days went by, and the police had come to investigate the house after she hadn't reported to work and officially declared Mrs. Kraus as missing. They didn't find any evidence to suggest foul play. This is morbid, but I felt better after hearing that, even though we had killed our teacher. I mean, how could we do that? To this day, I still don't understand how Lester talked all of us into doing that.

Lester wanted to go to her property now that the police were gone. He wanted to check on the body. It was close to the river but shouldn't have been close enough to have been swept away from the floodwaters. We walked to the spot, only to our horror, the hole was emptied, not by flood waters, but by something that had dug it up, stones and all.

"Oh crap, dude! The police did find her! We're screwed! We're going to jail! I'll never see my family again!" I screamed.

"Shut up!" Lester demanded.

"We're never getting out! This is it! We're done!" Kevin started crying.

Jordan just sat on the ground and was weeping on his knees. "Let's check out her house," Lester declared.

"Why? What good would that do?" Kevin asked.

"Maybe whoever dug her up is there," Lester suggested, "It wouldn't hurt."

We walked back down to her house. The garage's back door was wide open—mud streaked all over the floor to the open door inside the house. We followed the trail of mud into the living room. There, her body was spread out across the floor, and on top of her corpse, her muddy cats were feasting.

Lester started laughing harder than I'd heard anyone laugh in my life.

Lester was laughing so hard that he had trouble breathing. He continued to laugh like that as the rest of us made haste to get out of there.

The next day, a massive flash flood swept the river, taking Mrs. Kraus's house with it. The police found her body miles down the river a few days later and classified her as a victim of the flooding. Her house wasn't far from the riverbank, so it was completely gone—evidence and all.

That was the last we ever saw of Lester. His house was empty, and I realize now, in writing this horrible story down, that we never met Lester's parents. The few times I had been to his house, I'd heard his mom but never actually seen her. It's pretty odd to think about now.

Not long after that, I started seeing this strange, golden cat with the freakiest green eyes. It never wandered very close to me, even if I offered it food. I would see it randomly, like on the school playground and sitting outside my bedroom window. It was always staring at me. I saw it outside before I walked in my front door, thirty miles from the town I grew up in.

The strangest part is that I walked past his house a few days after Lester disappeared and noticed it was empty. The walls were barren, and the paint and carpets were faded. The front door was unlocked, so I had to investigate. There was no evidence that anyone had lived there for a long time.

It also smelled like cat piss and the pungent, lingering odor of rotting meat.

GIVE IT SOME COLOR

I SPENT THE BETTER PART of a decade traveling up and down the East Coast, performing in front of crowds as small as fewer than a dozen people to crowds of thousands. I busted my body and ruined relationships for the chance to appear on TV and become rich. None of that ever happened. You see, something horrible happened to me one night that would result in the end of my career as a professional wrestler and the beginning of my career as a professional addict. That wouldn't be the end, though; I later found a way to seek my revenge. The following names will be fake because I'm not an idiot and won't incriminate myself for what I did.

It was October 2019, and I was booked to wrestle a veteran who went by Bulldog Bob. He was a third-generation wrestler, and his lineage went back to the carny days of the traveling circus. By the time I was set to face him, he was running a wrestling promotion, and due to a lack of sufficient talent, he had become the champion with a reign going on over three years. Bulldog Bob still ran things in old carny ways and was notorious for ripping off talent he didn't believe had earned it. I had been lucky, and Bulldog Bob usually paid me a little extra. You'll see why.

That night was not unlike any other. Before the show, I'd shower, talk to the other people backstage, and eat the customary hotdogs and soda. All this was to show the other people that I wasn't some asshole who thought of himself as too good to be there. I genuinely didn't believe I was and was just glad to live my dream. Bob and I stood behind the curtain as the match before ours unfolded.

"Now, here's what I want tonight. We have to amp this up. The crowd is bored to tears. Look at them! It's been the shits all night! We're going to give it some color tonight, Anthony. Ya, hear me?"

By color, he meant that I was going to bleed. The match would be a little more hardcore than the others, and this would be the climax of an awful card. All of this would result in that extra cash I told you about earlier. I was always bold about going the extra mile to impress the crowd and maybe even the promoter. No matter what I had to do, I would become a big name on TV with tons of merchandise, and kids would scream out my catchphrases every time they saw me.

After the previous match had concluded without much of a crowd reaction, the announcer informed the crowd that due to animosity backstage, our match was changed to a No Rules Match, which meant we could incorporate weapons. The match started with Bob throwing a cheap haymaker and connecting with my ear. That immediately pissed me off. We locked up, and Bob whispered into my ear that he popped, "had to give you some motivation, kid. Let's give 'em something to talk about tomorrow!"

Bob and I exchanged blows for several minutes, none being faked. I could feel my left eye swelling, but it didn't bother me. I'd had many injuries in that career, a black eye being one of the most common. At least with a black eye, you could keep working without stopping. It wasn't like a broken arm or leg; you could easily have a match with one swollen, purpled eye.

Several minutes into the match, it was time to turn up the heat. The crowd was roaring, and many were on their feet, and now was the opportune time to amplify their excitement.

Bob rolled out of the ring and retrieved a trash can that he quickly filled with implements he planned on us to inflict pain on each other. I was laid out in the ring, out of breath from the brawl, while Bob dragged the trash can through the ropes and dumped the weapons about the ring. After Bob whacked me across the ribs with a hockey stick, I rolled over in pain but grabbed a pool cue that I used to nail him between the legs in his nether region. Bob keeled over in agony, something the crowd riotously cheered me for. Bob had gained infamy for cheating his way to victories during his reign as champion, and the crowd absolutely hated him.

"You fucked up! You fucked up!" cheers rang out from the crowd. Hearing the crowd get into your match like that is a more considerable high than any drug I've tried, and that list is long.

As Bob lay there in agony, I went for the trash can and slammed it into his back, making him collapse onto the mat. I went for   the   pin.

He kicked!

Bulldog Bob was a tough old son of a bitch, and all that chaos wouldn't be enough to take the title from him. If someone were to beat him, they'd have to fucking earn it. He waited for me to argue with the ref that it was really a three-count when he put me into a hold from behind and drew a razorblade across my forehead. As he clutched me on the mat, he said, "Thanks for the color, kid. The crowd loves this shit". Blood immediately poured down my face, the hot, sticky liquid stinging my eyes and dripping into my open mouth, filling it with that tangy, metallic taste that only blood has.

I looked at the audience and saw little kids staring at me in panic, worrying about their good guy wrestler in the clutches of the ultimate evil guy, Bulldog Bob. Seeing those kids sparked the energy I needed, and I shook off old Bob. I popped Bob multiple times, sending the crowd into a cheering madness. Dazed by the blows, Bob stepped on a baseball bat and flew over the top rope to the floor on the outside, his body making a loud, meaty smack as he hit pure concrete below. That wasn't intentional.

Bob landed hard on his back, clearly hurt. I saw him rolling around in agony, reaching for his spine as he gnashed his teeth.

The ref and I jumped outside to check on him. Bob lay there, not moving. I heard him tell the ref that he was ok to continue, so I got back into the ring for the ref to count, giving Bob time to recover. During the nine-count, Bob sprang to life, jumped back into the ring, and was pissed off.

His face was blood red, and I could tell it wasn't from the fall. "That was all your fault, you little prick!" he yelled, inches from my face. The next thing I knew, he drew back and drilled me right between the eyes with brass knuckles.

I woke up in a hospital bed several hours later. My head was pounding, and I had twenty-five stitches on my forehead. Bob had punched me in the same place he had cut me with the razor earlier in the match, nearly splitting my scalp from my face. The bruising and swelling as it healed was indeed a sight to see. The top half of my face resembled an eggplant, shaped like a strange purple lump. I also started to have other complications after. The blow damaged my brain, causing me to have seizures for the first time. I was no longer healthy to compete, and thus, my career in the ring was over. In that instant, my life was shattered like a boulder through a house of glass.

I found out that Bob had escaped jail time by pleading that it was an accident in the ring, that I was supposed to move, but was a dumb rookie who couldn't work. This infuriated me. Not only did he end my career, but he was now trying his best to tarnish it. The police hadn't even asked for my testimony, so it felt safe to say they were in Bob's pocket. This began my descent into the bottomless hell of depression.

The next few weeks were an escalation of prescribed medication and self-administered. I started moping, drinking away my troubles instead of finding a real solution. I found a job stocking at a warehouse close to my apartment, which was enough to pay the bills with a little extra left over for booze. It started with drinking a few beers after work, to drinking a twelve-pack. It became horrible if I watched wrestling that night. The memories and realization that I could never do that again kicked my depression into overdrive, and I used booze to silence the sadness.

A guy I worked with, a tattooed skinny dude named Nate, introduced me to the resounding, winding hell of heroin. It wasn't long before I was getting fucked up instead of going to work, and every vein in both arms was blown out. Due to unpaid rent, I was also kicked out of my apartment. The same day, when I tried to clock in to work, my boss told me to "get the fuck out of here, junkie." I did walk into work pretty out of it from a high I was coming off of, so that was not surprising.

I spent the next four years bouncing between minimum—wage jobs and whatever house I could crash in. My family has forsaken me, as I was nothing but a useless bum in their eyes. I had gone from being goaded by them to being a black sheep in record time. This only fueled my drug abuse. It escalated quickly after that, resulting in several ODs, and the only thing that saved me was Narcan. Sometimes I would even get clean, going as long as a few months, but then something shitty would happen, and I'd go right back to the horse, and nearly every time, I'd overdo the dosage in my eagerness and OD again. Part of me wished that I would die. What was the point of living if I couldn't do what I loved or be surrounded by those I loved?

The junk put me in such a haze that, one day, I was walking to my job at a fast-food restaurant when I saw Bob walk out of the same building. I had no idea where Bulldog Bob lived, but now I knew where he liked to eat. An idea formulated in my mind, inspired by an incinerating hatred that bubbled up from deep within my wounded soul. Not only did Bob end my career, but the son of a bitch never even apologized. Not once did he even speak to me after the fact. He must've genuinely believed that I deserved what I got for something he thought I did to wrong him.

I did some careful research and discovered Bob's home address. That was when my plan came to fruition. I decided that I was going to kill Bulldog Bob. It would've been easy to find someone to do it for me. I hung around shady types every single day, and I'm sure one of them knew someone who knew someone, but I wanted to do this myself. This was personal. Bob had taken everything from me, and I would take it from him, too.

Bob lived on a piece of secluded property outside of town.

Forest surrounded the property on three sides, and only the front and driveway were clear. It disgusted me how well off he was. This sick, twisted old man who had screwed over countless other ignorant up-and-coming wrestlers over the years was living in a house that I would consider palatial. It was a three—story Victorian-style home with a wrap-around porch, perfect for that old piece of shit to enjoy what he had stolen. It was enough to make me want to vomit.

After camping out in the surrounding forest for two weeks, I decided that I knew his routine well enough to start my plan. I realized that Bob lived alone, and no other person visited the home in those two weeks. Bob also had no dogs and no security system. The dumb old prick probably thought he was safe living out in nowhere. It was just too perfect.

It was too easy to sneak into his house, find his bedroom, and stand over him as he snored like a suffocating bear. The duffel bag full of my tools was lying next to my feet. I carefully opened it and whacked him right across the forehead with a wooden baseball bat. When he awakened, he was bound to a chair in his basement. He tried to talk, but the tape and dirty sock I had stuffed in his mouth muffled his voice; it was my sock and hadn't been washed in probably several months.

The last few weeks had given me time to think about what I would say and do to the old bastard. This had to be perfect in every way. My revenge would not only be satisfying, but gratifying in every way. I approached Bob, who sat below the only light in the basement. The baseball bat bounced in my palm as if it were the metronome for what was about to occur.

"Bob, you may not remember me, but I used to wrestle for you. You always told me I was reliable and a good worker, but one day, you decided to punch me out with brass knuckles because you thought I had gone into business for myself. Do you remember me now, Bob?"

Bob's eyes looked angry momentarily, but then I saw the moment the memory set in. He did remember me. Fear spread across his face as he said something else muffled, probably an empty apology or some shitty excuse for what he did. With everything my drug-addled body could summon, I punched the carny prick on the bridge of his nose; blood poured down his face in a stream. I could hear him make a muffled cry, which excited me.

For my next trick, I dug through my Duffle Bag of Doom and found a set of brass knuckles. The light bounced off the shiny metal in a spectacular sparkle, almost as if it were excited about what would come.

"Do you remember now, Bob? In case you somehow don't recognize me. You may not, because I've been doing heroin for several years. Most of my teeth are gone, my muscles all withered away, yet you still live in luxury. Do you know how sick that is, Bob? I couldn't cope with not living my dream anymore, and my family abandoned me because of what I'd become! Do you know how sick that is, Bob? Do you?"

I grabbed the back of his balding head and pounded his forehead repeatedly with the brass knuckles. Eventually, the muscle connecting his forehead to his scalp began to split. I dug my fingers into the crease and pulled. A sickening wet rip came as I pulled his scalp away from his flesh. Bob shrieked through the dirty sock the entire time, shaking uncontrollably. I could even smell the unmistakable odor of piss and shit. Once his bald scalp was peeled to the back of his head, I took out a hunting knife and cut it away, then dropped the flap of flesh onto his lap.

"This is only part of what you deserve, you sick old fuck! Think about all the others you've ripped off, the careers you've ruined, the reputations forever tarnished! Think about all that while I do this next."

I took the brass knuckles and punched the exposed flesh under the scalp. The meaty thump of each blow splashed Bob's hot blood onto my face and into my mouth. Soon, his head resembled ground beef instead. I jumped off the chair and marveled at my masterpiece. I could feel the blood splatter on my face mixing with my sweat as it ran into my eyes, nose, and down my tattered old shirt. After not being in ring shape for years, I was gassed.

"You wanted some color, Bob. Now you fucking have it!"

I removed the baseball bat from the duffel bag for the finale. I never played baseball in school, but I wouldn't be hitting that type of ball. Like a battering ram, I gripped the bat with both hands and nailed him square in his shriveled old manhood. He doubled over; the breath sucked from his lungs in a quick gasp. The bat flipped upward, and I delivered multiple blows to each knee.

Sweat soaked my body now, and I could feel the urge to get high setting in quickly.

"Now, Bob. Do you think you can still compete? How's that for a no-rules match?"

The ball bat cracked across his forehead with a knockout blow. This match I had won. I was the new champion.

Champion of what? The champion of revenge. I left that house feeling like a brand-new man. The sunshine outside felt brighter than it had in a very long time.

Following the incident, I checked myself into rehab, and I've been clean since. I no longer had a reason to live inside the fog. Getting clean wasn't easy and never is. I was convinced that the withdrawals would kill me, but once they had passed, I contacted my family a few states over and moved in with them. We've been on excellent terms since.

As for Bob, I saw his story on the news a few weeks later. Someone had found him days later, a business partner who had come over to discuss buying out another promotion. I imagine that the police never had any leads because Bob had made so many enemies over the years. As far as I know, that case hasn't been solved.

TELL ME A STORY

IT WAS A RESTLESS NIGHT; my brain was too stressed to allow me to sleep. Relentless tossing and turning had succeeded in keeping sleep away from me. Facebook and Reddit kept my brain occupied, only relieving a small amount of the stress. This happens to me way too often.

My closet door started rattling. Slow at first and then violently, like something huge was behind it. A large, furry beast burst out of the doors, pushing them apart in a great lunge. It was the monster from my childhood, returning to torment me some more.

The monster's hairless face glared at me, only charcoal skin and a mouth of a hundred-pointed teeth. There were no eyes, just hollow black holes.

"Tell me a story," the monster asked in its deep, distorted voice.

"A—a story?" I replied, cowering under my blankets.

"Yes. Just like when you were little. I want a story! Tell me a story!"

"O—okay. Uhm. Let me think of something."

"Hurry! I must have a story! Oh, and make it scary! I love to be scared!" it said to face me straight as it plopped its big furry bottom on the edge of my mattress, the springs letting out a squeaky sigh as it sank.

And this is the story I told the monster that night. "It was a dark and stormy night…"

"Boo! Start over!"

"What? Really?"

"Yes! Too cliché! I don't want to sleep; I want to be scared!"

"Okay, okay. Sheesh. I'll start over."

The big beast adjusted himself on the bed t. It stretched and plopped back down on the bed. The curved horns on its head were close to the ceiling when it stood up.

"I am ready when you are, little human."

"They told us it would be all right, and we would never have to be afraid again. The evil man, known as Hook Hand by us kids, was dead. Children had been reported for weeks, and the police finally went to his home, and he was shot dead after trying to put up a fight. We had no reason to fear going outside again."

"Oh! This is a good one! Keep it up!"

"Then, one night, they found Joey Smith, who lived down the road from me. Well, they found pieces of Joey."

"Oh fudge!" the beast screamed as he dove under my bed, raising it in the air a few feet.

"What are you doing? Jesus!"

"I'm not Jesus!"

"I didn't..."

"Keep going! This is getting good!"

"Well..." I said as I tried to balance myself, "Joey wasn't the only one. A few nights later, they found Halie McDonald dead in her room, ripped from her chin to her navel."

"Oh my God! Not a little girl!"

"Yes. True story. She was a classmate of mine."

"Were there others?"

"Yes. My little brother, Donnie. We found him a few days after Halie. Same thing as her, too."

"Did they ever figure out what happened to them? Please tell me they did!"

"Nope. Some say that Hook Hand is still alive to this day." The lights went out without warning. I saw the outline of a man open my bedroom door and slowly walk in. He had a hook for a hand.

"What happened? Who is that?"

"It's Hook Hand. He's finally going to fix this problem forme."

"No!"

The beast darted from under my bed to the closet, and the doors slammed hard behind it. Hook Hand disappeared, laughing menacingly. We have had this deal worked out for a long time.

"What's the matter? I thought you liked being scared!" I said to the monster, laughing as it ran like a coward.

***

Joey bullied me for years, shoving me in the dirt at recess, taking my lunch and eating it in front of me, and yanking my shorts down in front of the girls.

Good riddance.

And Halie? She was the girl that broke my heart.

My little brother? He was an annoying little shit who cried all the time, and my parents always favored him more.

Do I regret any of it? No.

The ritual to summon Hook Hand back from the dead was tedious, but I can't undo it now. So, to keep him from killing me, I sic him on others. That monster has been showing up randomly for decades. I could never time it right, but this time, I got him.

He'll never bother me again.

THE MAN WITH RED EYES

HE'S BEEN WATCHING me. Just staring and staring. I don't know who he is or what he wants with me, but I wish he would go away. There he is. Everywhere I look and in everything I walk past with a glass surface. I hope you can help me.

Let me explain. It started last week. The landscaping company I work for was hired to mow the grass, trim the hedges, and wash the windows of this office building in the older part of the city.

No big deal.

We had done hundreds of jobs like this over the years. I assumed this one would be the same old song and dance.

The other workers were assigned to mow, trim, and clean while I cleaned all the windows. I had made it to the third-floor windows, feeling exhausted. Typically, I don't mind cleaning the bird shit and bug guts off the windows, but today, the sun reflected continuously into my face. It felt like being inside of a microwave oven.

I have a method for the cleaning process—spray, start from the top by swiping to the left, right, and left again in a large S shape, usually taking about 30 seconds to clean a window.

The third-floor windows seemed to have a hundred windows, but there were only twenty-five. When I was at the fifth window, I needed to change to my last spray bottle. I turned and grabbed the bottle sitting in the caddy attached to the basket. Just as I was about to turn back around, a man was standing in the window.

Let me state that no one was standing there before. He glared at me; his eyes were bulging, bloodshot, and ringed with dark red circles of anger.

He was an older, bald man with gray tufts of hair on the sides. His business attire made me think that maybe he worked there. I noticed that the man's eyes were full of rage and hatred, and his hands were balled into white-knuckled, veiny fists. Fear began to run through me. I didn't know what to do. I turned around to look for one of my co-workers, but none were around. They had finished their duties and were relaxing in the air conditioning of our work trucks. I fumbled for my cell phone, but I dropped it through the cracks of the lift basket, and I heard it smack onto the concrete below.

After thinking and debating, I returned to finish cleaning the window. I figured if the man was there, he couldn't get through anyway because office windows are typically sealed shut. The man was still standing there, but now he was closer and screaming something at me. I couldn't hear what he was saying, and I don't mean he was inaudible, but it was as if there was no sound coming out of his mouth. I heard him just fine moments before, but I suddenly heard nothing. I decided that it was best to go about my job, and I sprayed the window. The man went insane then. He started pounding his fists on the window, screaming even harder, but I could hear him now.

"Get away from me! Get away! I've been disturbed! You awakened me!"

His knuckles were bleeding, but he continued to assault the window. I couldn't back up any further than I had, so I scrambled to lower the lift. The edges of the window started to budge. I saw bits of the brick façade crumble as he pounded and pounded. I was panicking by this point. Behind me, I saw one of my co-workers casually walking across the parking lot toward the parked trucks.

"John! Hey, John! What the hell is going on up there?"

I turned back around, and the man was gone now. The seal of the window was fine, and the window was pristine, sparkling in the sun as if I had waxed it instead. The man was nowhere to be seen, and the blinds were closed. I stared at the window for a while, trying to analyze what had happened, when my co—worker started yelling back.

"Hey, John! What's wrong?"

"Nothing! My pulley was stuck, but I got it!"

"Okay! Well, hurry up because we all want to grab some burgers!"

After finishing the rest of the windows in record time, we stuffed ourselves with burgers and beer. I went home, greeted by my cat. It was her dinner time, after all.

"Here, Pirate. I know; you're starving," I said to her while petting her round belly.

After grabbing another beer from the fridge, I planted myself in the recliner and clicked on my TV. Being single has its advantages sometimes. Pirate jumped on the couch and went to sleep almost in an instant. I would pay a hefty sum of money to live her life.

The local news told me the same things I had always heard; car wrecks, more people dying from narcotics addictions, and the economy sinking further into the shitter as always. I was taken from my comfort zone by my door, pounded by heavy thumps. It was my neighbor, Abe. He was older, but sometimes he'd come over for drinks.

"Hey, Abe. What's going on?"

"John, did you hear?"

"No?"

"They found Sonny this morning. They said he was dead in his kitchen. The cop who interviewed me said his face was frozen in terror like he had been scared to death! They interviewed everyone while you were at work to see if we knew anyone who had it out for him. I don't think they told anyone else about it, but I have my ways of charming people. They said there were no signs of forced entry, but they did notice something odd. There were handprints on his back window. That's a fifteen-foot drop with no way to get there, John. How the hell? Did they bring a huge ladder just to off the guy?"

"Beats me, but I'll keep an eye out. I got an extra pistol in the back if you need one."

"I'm good, man. The last thing I need is a pistol that's not registered to me," he laughed and patted me on the shoulder, "I'll hit ya up for a beer sometime soon."

"Fridge is always stocked."

It was later that night that I decided to head to bed. It was Friday night, and I was feeling rebellious. Besides, I had run out of shows on Netflix that piqued my interest. I told Pirate goodnight, patted her on her graying head, and started toward the bedroom.

Thump Thump Thump

"Let me in!"

It was coming from my back window. The hairs all over my body immediately stood up. I felt the absolute worst feeling of my life from hearing that voice. I knew immediately who it was, too.

That window is situated in the back of my kitchen beside the fridge. It offers a nice view of the city park, and it's nice to look out of while you drink coffee in the morning. Instead of seeing the old oaks in the park, I now see that old man with his bloodshot, red eyes staring at me.

He didn't say a word—he just stared at me, never blinking.

Thump Thump Thump

I ran into my room to get my pistol. Pirate darted past me and dove under the bed, and I couldn't really blame her. I retrieved the pistol from the drawer on my bedside table and popped the clip in. When I came back to the window, he was gone. On my window, there were handprints, just like Sonny's.

I didn't realize the connection then, but now I do. A few days before the office job, we had been hired to clean up the local graveyard after a nasty series of storms rolled by, strung tree branches and debris all over the place, and overturned some headstones, creating a huge mess there. I was trying to dig out the drainage ditch of loose debris when I started a few feet away from where it actually was. That's how bad of a mess we were dealing with.

"John! Stop!" my supervisor called over as he ran toward me.

"What's wrong?"

"Man! You just started digging up a grave!"

"Sorry, Ralph! My bad!" I said as I looked around, trying to ascertain where I was.

"Now you're gonna be haunted!" Ralph said, laughing at me sarcastically, on the verge of nudging me in the ribs.

I see the red-eyed man every day, sometimes multiple times a day. He appears on the windows of cars, mirrors, and still on the windows I clean at work. Sometimes, he doesn't say a word; other times, he yells.

"I was sleeping so well! Why did you wake me? Why?"

I often request not to clean the windows at work now to limit the times that I see the screaming man.

"Why not, John?" my boss asked me the first time. I had thought up a lie the night before. I wasn't about to tell him the truth about why I didn't want to clean the windows. Tell him that the ghost of a crazy, red-eyed old man who screams at me in the windows would probably get me committed.

"The glare gives me migraines."

"Alright, sure. Why didn't you tell us this before?"

"I tried to just work through it. I bought sunglasses and ibuprofen, but none seems to help."

"You should go see your doctor then. Maybe they can give you something to help."

Yeah, I'll see a doctor so that they can throw me in the nuthouse.

I can hardly sleep because I'm always dreaming of him, dreaming of his red eyes and that blood-curdling yell. The windows in my apartment are all covered in black trash bags, and I've taken all the mirrors and picture frames down in the apartment—I even gave my coffee table with the glass top away to Goodwill. I've done all that I can do to keep my sanity while I'm at home. It's been close to a year since this began.

I don't know what else to do. I'm writing this down because I hope someone can help me, or it's going to drive me insane.

DEAR MOTHER

DEAR MOTHER, I AM FINE.

Please, don't worry about me. I'm only a convicted murderer, after all. There is no need to worry about me. Pain is only a fragment of what I deserve for my deeds, and of those, I couldn't give a damn.

Some idiot thought he could catch me in the shower a few days after I was dropped here like a bag of trash instead of a human. I broke his neck in front of the other inmates to show them that I was not afraid. No one has messed with me since. Here I am, locked inside this cement coffin, rotting away like the piece of shit they think I am.

I find myself with a lot of free time. I'm sure you're not surprised by that. Much of that time has been spent dwelling on the past. Do you know how painful that is? To be locked away, thinking of times that I was actually happy, and to know that I will never feel that way again?

I remember one particular even when I was a small child, back when my grandmother was alive. I remember her yelling, "Clara Dolly Epps!" at you like you were still a child to her. I wonder if he would feel ashamed or proud to know that her grandson killed six women just to get a woman to have sex with him and not say no? Would she enjoy knowing how I gutted them like a dead fish after I finished the deed? How did I leave them all to the animals deep in the woods? How do I have little feelings for the lives of other people? I'm sure she would love it.

What about Dad? Have you heard from him? Probably not, since that bastard ran away in '94. Remember that? We woke up one morning, and he was gone. You had to work three jobs, including blowing guys for five bucks behind the motels. You didn't know that I knew that, did you? I suppose you don't care if I do or not.

Did you know that I still feel the urge to kill? Right now? If I had the chance, my last kill would be myself. I am a miserable piece of shit, sitting on my concrete slab, with nothing to look at but a blank television set from probably 1984 and my little metal shit can in the corner. Sometimes, I get so bored I take a shit just because I have nothing else to do. I'm sure you wanted to know that. Right, Mother?

Oh, Mother. I forgot. You won't ever read this. Remember how I slit your throat from ear to ear? What was that last thing I said to you? Oh right.

"Smile, bitch!"

I'm sorry. I made myself laugh. I apologize, Mother. You hateful, sour, bitter, old hag. I hope you're burning in hell. I know I will. I look forward to seeing you, Mother. It's not long now until they finally inject me with the Justice of God Juice, or whatever those looney, uptight people on the news like to say.

I hope that whoever gets this or reads this will remember one thing—I regret nothing. During the last fifteen years or so, I'm sorry that I lost count after staring at blank, gray walls every single fucking day. I've had plenty of time to contemplate. I thought maybe if I thought harder and harder, I might become like a normal person and feel bad for all that I've done. I can't say that I feel a goddamn thing. In fact, sometimes, it gets me hard thinking about what I did, about how I wish I could do it again. I'd love to do it again, for old times' sake.

Oh, Mother. How I miss you. I miss your abuse. I miss the cigarette burns on my arms. I miss being punched unconscious by your boyfriends, my tiny head bouncing off the gravel outside our trailer. Maybe that's why I'm so fucked up? Did you ever stop to consider how this would affect me? Probably not.

All you cared about was what you could get out of them, and then you'd throw them away once they weren't useful to you anymore.

I've done many things I should regret but don't. There is one thing that I do regret, Mother. I regret the deal. I regret that demon I met. I regret selling him my soul. Why did I do it, Mother? Well, it was revenge, pure and simple. I wanted to get even; I wanted to avenge my lost childhood and my sanity.

Who was my first victim, Mother? Do you remember Jack?

The large Black man with the fists the size of bowling balls? Those fists would pummel me daily until you finally had the sense to get rid of him. I don't believe they ever found his remains, but they had enough evidence to convict me. How delightful! I bashed his head in with a tire iron that I had in the trunk of my car. Finding a bag large enough for his massive remains was difficult, so I had to chop him up like a thick, juicy steak. He's resting at the bottom of Lake Superior somewhere now.

And Benny? Do you remember him? The brainless junkie with the swastika tattoo on his neck? I think that was your 'Bad Boy Phase.' They found his head in Michigan and his torso in Wisconsin. You have no idea how much I loved it. Watching him squirm while I cut his legs off while he squirmed in agony, the pain making his body quake in seizure fits.

Let's not forget my favorite boyfriend of all. He was difficult to track, but I found him hiding in Pittsburgh. Good ol' Kevin Bishop. Remember him? He was missing the pinky on his left hand from a bar fight, a story he would tell every single goddamn day. He was the one who bounced my head off the gravel and gave me forty-five stitches. Do you remember that? I ran his head over with his car, which made a satisfying, wet pop. I found an old, abandoned mine shaft a good drive from Pittsburgh and chucked his body in there. I wish his car was small enough to fit, too, but oh well.

Then there were the women. I mainly targeted the ones who made fun of me in school. I didn't tell you much about those because you were too strung out to care about anything but your next fix by then. They made fun of my deformed nose.

Remember that? When Benny punched me in the face with brass knuckles because I told him to stop pulling my hair? That's what I get for defending my junkie of a mother. It was five all together. They all got their equal share.

It's a shame that the last one escaped.

The lawyer didn't even have to ask for me to plead guilty—I did it anyway. I felt no shame, and I told the judge that. I had to do it. I'm glad that I did. Are you happy now, Mother? Now that I've told you all about my dirty deeds? I wonder if you would even care.

Once again, dear Mother, don't worry about me.

I am fine.

I will see you soon.

THE SUMMONING OF BLOODY BONES

IN 1848, BOONE COURT House, West Virginia, was nothing but a logging town and a collection of farms. It would later be named Madison in 1906, but right now, that was a far-off dream. The sparsely populated backwoods had fewer than thirty-five hundred people living within its newly appointed boundaries, and one family had just recently settled there. Elizabeth McComas and her family, a group of second-generation Scotch—Irish immigrants searching for a new life and hideaway, moved down this way from the northern part of the undivided state of Virginia. You see, she didn't come from a lineage of ordinary immigrants. No, they were what some would call 'mountain witches.' Their ways and knowledge had been passed down for untold generations, and Elizabeth was only the most recent to learn their teachings.

She was sixteen this year, and her womanhood began a few years prior. She was what most would say was a woman grown by then. There had been offers from would-be suitors, many old enough to be her father and one old enough to be her grandfather, but Daddy had deemed those boys not good enough for his little Liz, nor was she ready. Her Mama was still teaching her their ways. Liz could whip up most medicines and find most of the herbs in the surrounding woods in no time flat, but she still hadn't mastered the art of hiding. Keeping their true gifts hidden was important for her people, and if she were to pass the ways down to the next generation, she'd have to master this first.

One morning, Liz whipped up a concoction of several herbs, ground them into a fine powder, and mixed them with her morning urine. When she went to bathe in the nearby creek that evening, why it didn't surprise her when handsome Johnny Ballard found his way over to her. He dumbly gazed at her nude body as she poured a bucket of water over her head, the streams cascading down her newly formed curves and tufts of hair. He was enthralled, but unbeknownst to him, he was also enchanted. At the snap of her fingers, he spun around and was on his way home, his young manhood at full salute the entire walk back.

Why, it was downright embarrassing when he walked into his family cabin in front of his brothers and parents like this. He couldn't exactly recall why or how he came to be like this or where he had even been. They didn't believe him, though, and he was punished with extra chores around the farm. The following evening, as he was gathering the day's chicken eggs, he found his mind wiped clean, and the only thought birthing amidst it was the urge to go back to that creek.

This time, though, he found Liz standing nude by the banks, her body already cleansed but waiting for him. They kissed, and their hands explored each other's changing bodies, but that was as far as Liz would let him go. She snapped her fingers, and he was off again, back to the farm and doing his chores, without remembering what had just transpired. Liz went home, feeling somewhat satisfied with herself and her newly found abilities. Not only was she born into that bewitched family, but she was also born with powers. She found out a long time ago that she could coerce the minds of those around her as long as they were weaker and ungifted. The creek was far enough from the family cabin that none of them were none the wiser to her doings.

Liz did this every night for weeks until she allowed Johnny to remember. She had a secret crush on this strong farm boy for years. The main road out of the holler they lived in passed right by his farm into town. One morning, she saw him toiling out in the field, with his shirt long cast away in the summer sun, the long hoe he chopped into the ground with exaggerated blows as he knew she watched. She, indeed, was watching and not hiding the fact. She stared longingly at his strained muscles; the sweat sparkling off his tanned skin, his long hair blowing around like the leaves in the tree when the breeze blessed him with some relief from the heat. Liz might've been drooling, but she knew she had to hurry to town before the general store ran out of flour.

That wasn't the first time she had noticed Johnny. They had gone to church together at the Trinity Fellowship Baptist Church.

Johnny always sat on the front bench with his Pappy, Deacon Bartholomew Ballard. Deacon Ballard was a staunch disciplinarian, even with his wife. He wasn't afraid to boast about laying a hand or two on his wife if she deserved it.

Because he was the deacon, most of the tiny population wouldn't speak up to him except Jacob McComas, Liz's father. He refused to step foot in that place until the deacon was "thrown on his ass," as he liked to say. Instead of church, Jacob would commune in the woods with his Bible on his lap and one of his wife's teas sitting nearby. He believed nature was closer to God and the spirit world than a square building with benches.

Johnny was one of the boys Jacob had shooed away from Liz, saying he would be a wife-beater just like his God-forsaken daddy. Her daddy had always been nice to her mama, treating her as close to an equal as possible for that time. Liz admired and loved him for that, and her mama loved him even more. If there was such a thing as soulmates, it was them, and she longed for that connection. Something stirred in her soul and said that Johnny was hers, and she would make that happen come hell, high water, or anything in between.

One evening, as she embraced Johnny down by the creek, she stripped Johnny down nude as well; her teenage lust consumed her, and she considered lying down to let him take her innocence. That was when her daddy came down to the creek, bucket in hand, to get water for the goats. Daddy was enraged, beating Johnny within an inch of his life and declaring that Liz would not be allowed outside without supervision until she was married.

Johnny staggered home that day, beaten, and swore on his word he wouldn't come around Liz again.

Liz begged and pleaded with her daddy to let her marry Johnny, but he refused.

"That scum is not going to be your husband," he reaffirmed. "The man you will call a husband wouldn't bed a woman before marriage and, most certainly, not see her as naked as her birth!" She mourned for weeks, first trying a hunger strike, but this didn't last long before Mama slipped some herbs that caused her to be overcome by an uncontrollable hunger. When the strike didn't work, she tried to run away, but Mama had placed wards around the property that stopped her dead as if an invisible leash bound her by the ankles. In the end, Liz concluded that her home had become her prison. She had to find a way out.

Several weeks after she and Johnny were discovered, she found a book hidden in a chest. It was written in old Gaelic, but she was taught to read those texts. In it, she saw her solution. A wide smile spread across her face. She knew that soon she would have her freedom, and she would have Johnny. Liz couldn't be happier or even more anxious about the future.

The following morning, she and her sister Delilah were tasked with going into the woods to gather herbs for food and medicines to stock up before winter brought its snowy doom to the area. Winters here can be harsh; sometimes, one storm can dump several feet of snow. They'd be trapped inside for weeks as the only road out of their holler would be blocked off. Mama always stocked herbs if someone caught a chill or suffered hypothermia from the insufferably wicked cold winds.

Liz gathered other herbs secretly, stashed in a satchel tied to her thigh beneath her dress. That night, she was punished by being made to prepare supper for the family. Not much later, everyone slept like a babe with a belly full in a deep sleep. She headed to the mountaintop to start her ritual in the food she had sneaked in from the concoction she had slipped into everyone's food. She stacked wood into a triangle at the mountain's peak, and the flames breathed to life, reaching high into the sky as intended. First, she threw a ground mix of special ground herbs, mushrooms, and animal bones into the fire, then she threw a cup of her monthly blood into the flames, and last, she threw a note on which she wrote the name of the wicked Deacon Bartholomew Ballard over and over again.

The flames changed then. They shifted from long-reaching arms into a spiral, spinning around the kindling like a pinwheel. The inferno belched and spread, threatening to reach out to the greenery around them, but it never did. Through the raging flames, she could make out a figure forming. It was tall, probably eight feet if she had to swear by it, and it was ungodly skinny, too skinny, looking as if it were starving to death and unable to do as she desired. However, all those concerns washed away when they emerged from the fire.

It was indeed as tall as she thought. It was a massive skeleton of a man, drenched in the blood she had thrown into the fires to summon it. She had no idea how this creature could even move without crumbling into a heap, but she wouldn't question the magicks she hadn't learned yet. It stared at her while the fires behind it died down to cinders. Then it reared back and shrieked into the night sky. The creature dashed down the path she had used, heading toward Johnny Ballard's family cabin. She heard screams, gunfire, and other chaos you'd probably hear if a monster attacked someone's home. In the morning, the finale of her plan would come together. That night, she couldn't sleep a wink; she could only think about the future she had planned for her and Johnny.

When her parents roused from their sleep the following day, she ran into their rooms and announced that she and Johnny would be wed.

"What in the hell are you talking about, girl? I already said no, and I mean—" She cut her daddy off by raising her hand.

She replied, "But Daddy, that problem is taken care of."

"What do you mean, Liz? What did you do?"

"That wife beatin' daddy of his is not going to be a problem no more. Johnny can't learn to be a wife beater if he isn't around one! Best of all, you can go to church now, Daddy. Isn't that great?" Liz proclaimed with pride oozing from her voice.

"What did you do, girl?" her daddy reiterated. A tiny bit of terror was evident in his voice, coated by the fears of what he knew his wife was capable of, and therefore, Liz could as well. Their powers were great and terrifying, much worse than he'd heard in those stories his own mama told him as a little boy.

Those stories were just fables; this was real.

Jacob McComas threw on his boots and jacket, then ran into the dewy early in the morning of October. Down the road, he was greeted by an awful sight. He could see the blood before he even stepped foot on their property. The front door had been smashed in, lying on the floor of their cabin home in splinters. Strewn around the room were various body parts belonging to each member of the Ballard family: arms here, legs there, a head maybe, some features so destroyed you couldn't tell what it was supposed to be. The blood and viscera were sprayed on every inch of that room and everything within it. Jacob had seen carnage after field-dressing hundreds of animals in his life, even seeing the aftermath of a bear kill several times, but none of that was as gory as this was. Jacob stepped out of the cabin's threshold and emptied his stomach of last night's supper.

The problem for poor Liz is that she didn't specify on her list of who not to kill. Her ignorance of the ways and laws of magick cost her dearly. She had dived too deep and quickly into old ways without first learning. That was why her parents hadn't let her practice or get married yet. She had yet to learn discipline. Jacob came home and made the sad report. He regretfully informed young Liz that Johnny had been one of the victims but didn't say what he had seen. Johnny had been removed from all his limbs and head, which sat in the front yard, staring up at that morning's beautiful blue sky. Liz broke down and told them all that she had done.

Her Mama rushed to gather the ingredients necessary for the spell to cast that demonic beast back to Hell, where it came from. That night, she went to the same mountain peak, created a similar triangular pile of wood, and threw in the same ingredients, except, on her note, it was an incantation to banish the monster forever and ever, amen. Behind her, she heard the beast approaching through the thick overgrowth, but she continued. She had to read the spell thirteen times before casting it into the flames, but she only reached number seven. The beast snatched her from behind and cast her into the fire herself, along with the note, immediately making her vanish to the pits of Hell.

Luckily, Jane McComas had thought ahead and sent her daughters away to her sister's house across the river. She told her sister everything that would happen and what could happen and had prepared the correct wards to keep the thing away from their property. The beast never came for the McComas girls because it couldn't. Jacob also escaped, married another woman, and had more children with her, but this woman wasn't gifted in her ways. The McComas girls lived with their aunt for the rest of their childhood, learning under her experienced tutelage. Liz was married a few years later to a young beau named John Price. Some of you may even be descended from her. If you've ever had premonitions, dreams that came true, or swore you could sense a bad person, you may have inherited the gift.

They say, though, if you go off into those woods and wander the wrong direction, you'll run into ol' Bloody Bones yourself and be ripped asunder by his long, powerful arms. Parents now use the story of Bloody Bones to warn wayward children to listen and be good kids, but the truth is, it's out there and waiting for the chance to get you, too.

I HATE WORKING AS A SECURITY GUARD

WORKING AS A NIGHT SECURITY guard has its ups and downs. You spend a lot of time alone and with very little human interaction. That suits me just fine, to be honest. I usually lounge back, listening to either audiobooks or podcasts, and sometimes read a book. Horror is one of my favorite genres, but I never thought I'd live a real-life horror story.

I'll keep this short, so I'm sorry if the condensed version isn't up to par. It's difficult to shrink down an experience like this into only a few words. With my job, I'm stationed in a truck guarding an abandoned warehouse on a forgotten coal mine site that sits roughly three miles into the mountains of southwestern West Virginia. I've heard stories that odd creatures roam these woods at night. I witnessed an unfortunate fellow who found this lesson out the hard way.

I had parked in my usual spot, a few yards away from the bathroom entrance. Usually, I sit with the headlights on, hoping to scare off any would-be thieves with my presence. The mine was dug into a hillside, and they made a parking lot about thirty feet wide to accommodate the workers. The hill slope was preserved for the most part, so it had a nice, natural look to it. The hillside is covered in thick foliage during the summer months. I heard a noise loud enough to make itself known over the podcast I was listening to. A deep, vicious growl was coming from the brush near where I was.

I shined my flashlight in the general direction of where the sound was, and I saw gigantic red eyes flashback. A few moments later, a man dashed out of the bushes, trying to run across the parking lot down the hill toward an old dirt road. This is where the story gets crazy, but I will try to describe it to you as best as possible. A beast erupted from the bushes after the man. It had to be at least ten feet tall, maybe even twelve at the most. Its body was covered in thick black fur, and I could only see it thanks to my headlights. The beast tackled the man and assaulted him with a volley of massive claw strikes. I could hear the poor man screaming as his clothes were torn and his blood flew in all directions.

"Get off of me! Leave me alone!"

The beast only responded with growling and more strikes with its massive claws.

I thought about interfering, but what could I do? I had no weapon, and this thing could also take me down. So, I sat frozen, witnessing this horrific event. The beast paused to lick the blood and viscera from its claws, and that was when the man found the strength within himself to stand up and scurry down the hillside. I would say most people would be dead after an attack like that, but this man persisted. I knew that the hill led down to the main dirt road on the property, so I put the truck into drive and drove down there as fast as the piece of junk would take me.

At the bottom of the hill, I saw the blood trail going across the road, but I didn't see the man from a general observation. I wasn't about to get out of that truck, but instead, I sat in the truck for a while longer and waited. There is no cell service far into the middle of nowhere, so I'd have to radio the central office to call 911 if needed.

Several minutes went by, and I saw the beast again. It ran across the road and froze in front of my headlights. It stood there, staring at me, close enough to lay its hands on the hood of my truck, but it didn't. It just stared at me for a moment, then ran back up the hillside where it came from.

I didn't sleep for days after. The thoughts of that thing finding me and tearing me to shreds wouldn't leave my mind. I drank enough coffee the following nights that it should have killed me. I can't stop wondering if maybe, on a similarly horrific night, that creature will drag me out of the truck and eat me, too.

Maybe it would be better if I just quit that damned job.

THE CALL OF THE PIPER

I WOKE UP THAT NIGHT because I heard music. My first thought was that I left my phone on and connected to my Bluetooth speaker again, but the odd thing was that it wasn't music that I would typically listen to. Stumbling, I walked into the living room to check the speaker, but it was off. However, the music was louder in there. I peeped out the window and saw a short, odd-looking man strolling down the street, playing a flute in something close to a prance, like the old pictures of a satyr with their pipes.

He was wearing what appeared to be a long-tail coat and old hobnail boots. The melody reminded me of Danny Boy, but not quite the same; it was slower and in a minor key. My grandpa sang Danny Boy and would occasionally hum the tune, so I knew it well. The piper was playing a haunting, slow song, and it just sounded old—I don't know how else to explain it. I watched and listened until he turned the corner, and I couldn't hear the song anymore. Sleep was difficult to come by after that, but I managed to that night.

Nothing else strange happened for the next week, but the following week was when things turned south. My wife is a teacher at the local elementary school, and every day, she would come in and talk about more and more kids who weren't coming to school because of some unknown illness. She thought it was odd for that time of the year, but that happens with kids. The parents said they had just slept and only woke up to eat or use the restroom; then they would go back to bed and immediately fall into a deep sleep. The kids would not answer any questions or even acknowledge that anybody else was there. They just walked to the fridge in a trance-like state, grabbed something to eat, and walked back to bed.

By the end of the week, half of the student roster was out from this mysterious illness. The state school board shut the school down entirely for a quarantine. The story also found its way onto the local news, where they informed all of us that officials were clueless but were still investigating. The illness evolved shortly after. The students were now in a full-fledged coma, and the local hospital was filled with them by the end of the week.

The following week, the music woke me up again. It was the same weird song. That slow, minor tune drew me out of my sleep and toward the window again. Outside, I saw something alarming—kids were following the strange little man down the street like they were in a parade. It wasn't just a few of them—it was over a dozen. I counted for a bit, but stopped once the panic set in. I ran outside and started yelling at the kids to stop, but they weren't responding. The man was upfront, so I ran up to him, yelling, "Hey, creep! What are you doing, you…" That was all that I got out when he turned his head. Those sharp teeth and unhuman yellow eyes shut me up.

I realized who he was then. He was an exterminator. I couldn't remember his name and still don't, but I know that I had seen him around town in his ugly, puke-green van. It had a large logo across the side with bold letters that said.

PESTS B GONE! HAMLIN'S BEST TO KILL THE PESTS!

I work for the town, and I know that the town hired him after a recent flood caused a plague of rats to infest our city. He claimed he could get rid of them all in no time, as long as the town could pay. The town council obliged and said they would pay after the job was done, and he supposedly agreed to that. He actually single handedly took care of the rat problem in town.

I'm unsure how, but we no longer saw them scurrying every-where. Unfortunately, the council tried to weasel their way out of paying him.

"I'll get my payment, one way or another!" I heard him shout as he left the town hall after confronting them.

I ran as fast as I could back home to get my phone. The police came a few minutes later. I told them I saw the kids heading around the corner when I returned to get my phone. During the interview with them later, I told the story about the creepy man and told them about who I thought it was. They sent men around every part of town that night, checked all the possible places the creep could've been hiding them, and eventually got the names of all of them from the waking parents who were panicking about their missing children. The police told me they weren't sure of his name either, but it would be investigated. Alexia and I don't have children, but it still frightened us. Both of us had difficulty sleeping, and we were practically zombies for a few days.

The police acted and assigned officers to patrol the roads all hours of the night, every night. To their credit, I saw a car pass by every few minutes, which made us feel safe enough to sleep. The police issued a staunch warning to all parents to ensure their doors and windows were locked and to keep a vigilant eye on their children. At the end of the week, we heard about more children that had disappeared. The parents were enraged at the police officers for not seeing it or doing anything about it. The police claimed that their officers patrolled as instructed and did not report anything.

The following Saturday, the parents arranged for all the children to sleep in the local school gymnasium for that weekend, and the police chief agreed to have officers watching all the exits at all hours. Some of the parents even stayed to watch over their children. The school even tried to make an event of it by having games and food to keep the children distracted. When morning came, the parents discovered all the children that had stayed were missing. They also found all the police officers passed out on the floor near wide-open doors. The parents roused them by yelling and cursing them for letting their children go, but not one of the officers remembered passing out that night. The officers were all regular night shift patrollers, all well-acquainted with being up at odd hours during the night. Later that day, the police chief held a town meeting and stated he had the officers examined, and all the tests came back fine; none of them were under the influence of any substances or any signs of physical attack.

The parents demanded answers, and I can't blame them whatsoever. Some of them reached out to local news stations for more help. Our small town was swarmed with news trucks. On the local news, every night for weeks, a banner read "LIVE FROM HAMLIN." The news discovered that this also happened a few years prior in a small village in Germany. After weeks of children disappearing during the night, eventually, every child in the town vanished. Those children were never found, and not a single piece of evidence of their whereabouts was either.

The last incident occurred on the last Sunday of that horrible month. The police advised the parents that it may be safer to send their remaining children to relatives' homes in other towns for the time being. The parents agreed without argument. It was later reported that even those children disappeared.

My wife quit her teaching job to search for these missing children. She is now also missing. No one has found a sign of the children or my wife. After a few weeks, the news lost interest, and several suicide bombings in Europe broke their attention span. I've searched a thousand possible places in multiple towns nearby, but I've found nothing. The police also seem to have given up and stopped returning my calls. The last time that I went to the station, they arrested me for disorderly conduct because I refused to be told they couldn't or wouldn't help. I hope this post goes viral. Maybe that will finally get this story the attention it deserves, and these children and my wife can finally come home.

Please, will you help me?

I DIDN T DO IT

JOHN DAVIS MADE IT INTO town, barely able to move by then. The chilly weather had already come, but the snow hadn't fallen yet. The quiet little mountain town in the mountains of Montana was preparing itself for the oncoming winter. John had had a bad fever the day before he reached town, so he rented a room at the town inn and requested a doctor. The doctor saw him, immediately diagnosed him, and assigned his wife the task of checking on John from time to time. He stayed on that bed, sweating through piles of blankets, too weak to move.

The doctor and his wife were worried that he could die, but John Davis was a tough man. For the last twenty-odd years, he had roamed the untamed American West, collecting bounties and gold, but he never operated outside his morals. Out here, laws matter little to most men, so he did what he could to keep himself alive. He made an oath to himself that he would never kill anyone who didn't deserve it. He kept about two hundred dollars worth of gold in his hidden satchel for safekeeping. No one out here could know you had it, or you'd find yourself shot in the back. He intended on giving every piece of it to the inn and the doctor's wife if he lived through it. Bounties were easy to come by, and he could replenish it quickly.

The doctor's wife came in every thirty minutes, dabbing his forehead with a cold rag, feeding him stew, and went back to her routine of checking on other patients. She was gentle, with a touch that reminded him of his long-deceased mother. She was a brunette with dark green eyes, a resemblance very similar to his mother as well. John always smiled when she came in and thanked her when she finished. John Davis could never be rude to a pretty lady, after all.

A group of men rode into town, all bearing badges of the U.S. Marshals. They searched around town, looking for a wanted felon named John Davis. The group leader split them up and instructed them to search every building around town. Two of them decided it was better to get drunk at a tavern instead of looking for John.

"This is bullshit. I didn't like Sam anyway," said one of them.

The other man with him was already on his sixth beer while his friend had just finished his second.

"Damn straight. Fuck, Sam. He stole money from me while I was asleep! I'm glad he's dead. I don't know why Tom gives a rat's ass about him anyway."

"Because they were cousins, ya dumbass. How did you forget that?"

"I guess my memory's a bit fuzzy. Probably from this piss poor beer!"

"Probably also from all that damned drinking lately. What's gotten into you?"

"Nothin'," he responded, starting on another mug of beer.

After some searching around town, the other half of the group found out John was staying at the town inn. They stormed over to the tavern and found their other two intoxicated compadres.

"What in the hell has gotten into you two?" Tom, the leader of the group, said to them, "We got business to attend to you, and you're stinkin' drunk instead?"

"Sorry, boss. We miss Sam," Hank replied with slurred speech and reeking of booze.

"I don't give a shit! I brought you with me for a reason! Get up and get going before I shoot ya both!"

When they dragged the two drunks to the wagon, Tom commanded them to stay put until they returned. The group marched into John's room while he was receiving his twice-an—hour visitation.

"John Davis, you are under arrest for the murder of Sam Miller in Sioux Falls. I need you to come with us," the group leader informed him.

"Well, as you can see…" John tried to respond, but his voice was tired and raspy.

"He's not going anywhere. This poor man has been on the verge of death for days and is just now coming around. I can say that I hardly think of him as a murderer, sir. I think you may have the wrong man," the doctor's wife interrupted.

"We are not wrong, ma'am, and these types of situations aren't for women to be involved with."

"Just who the hell are you?" she snapped back.

"Tom Prescott of the U.S. Marshals. Now, who the hell are you to talk to a U.S. Marshall like that?"

"Emilia Smith is the wife of the doctor in this town. I kindly ask that you wait until we get him back to health before you drag him to jail. I won't have him dying on my watch." She was mad now. She had stood up, hands on her hips, right in the face of Tom Prescott.

Tom thought about it for a second and decided that he didn't need more trouble. "Alright. Very well. We will be staying here as well. I'll keep one of my men in here with him until he's… ready."

"Fine. Good day, Mr. U.S. Marshal," Emilia said, her face angry and stern.

Days went by, and John slowly recovered. He grew very fond of Mrs. Emilia and her kindness, but he knew nothing good would come of an attraction like that. He looked in the mirror—his face had grown a slight beard during his illness. Over the years, the chestnut brown of his youth had faded from his hair, and time had worn it down to a salt-and-pepper. The wrinkles were becoming more defined, and he started feeling old. Thankfully, his body didn't hurt too bad, minus the three places he had been shot.

He told Mrs. Emilia to leave the room for a bit so he could get dressed. He told the man guarding him when she walked out the door, "I'm ready when you are."

"You sure?"

"Yeah. Whatever you're accusing me of, I didn't do it. You'll probably just shoot me in the woods instead of a fair trial. Am I right?" John asked, his face showing no worry.

"You're acting so calm about it."

"I've been shot three times, nearly bled to death the second time. I'm not afraid of death; no sir, death is afraid of me."

They walked to the room where the Marshals were staying, with John shackled behind his back.

"All right, fellas. I don't know what you're accusing me of, but probably nothin' I can say will change your foolish minds."

"Very wise of you, but you know what you did. We'll get you to confess one way or another." Tom Prescott told him. "So, you'll be takin' me to the courthouse?"

"Nah. We've got other plans for you. No need for all that bull-shit," Tom said, sneering.

Well, shit, John thought. He considered running for it. All five of them were standing up now—all of them could draw their pistol and shoot him before he could even take two steps.

"C'mon, boys. We're done here." Tom commanded, his men snapping to attention in an instant.

One of the men tied a rope around John's shackles and yanked on them to move him along. He felt a bit like a cow, helplessly tied up, and being led to his untimely death. He grunted and swore under his breath every time they'd pull on that damn rope. Their wagon was parked not far from the inn.

Tom had one of the men haul John up into the back and threatened to shoot him if he tried to run.

"Don't worry. You won't see me running," he said.

John wondered how fast he could jump down and kill that man and then take his gun, but he decided that right then wasn't the time for such shenanigans. He stared at the inn as the horse—drawn wagon led him out of town. He waited to see if Mrs.

Emilia would come out and see him leave, but she didn't. He wasn't surprised. She was married, after all. Somehow, he still felt a ping of pain in his heart, just a small one, though.

Tom had one of his men sit back there with John in case he thought of doing something clever. Under other circumstances, John probably would have. John and the officer talked for a while, and John noticed the man kept belching very loudly, and it smelled like rot. John gagged, wishing his hands were free to cover his nose. After each belch, the man would pound his chest for a moment and complain about how much it burned.

The man was always chugging water or beer; if he wasn't do-ing that, he was eating food that he pulled from his bag. The beer didn't seem to intoxicate him at all. John counted the bottles in the back of the wagon at one point, and it totaled twenty-two, but the man was stone-cold sober. The man seemed to be like a furnace and burned off anything he consumed.

With nightfall coming, Tom Prescott ordered the driver to stop at a clearing in the forest up ahead.

"We stayed here the night before and had no trouble, so we'll stay here again," Tom explained to his cohorts.

Two men set up the tents, and the other two, including the belching man, lit a fire and cooked food.

"I hope that food doesn't attract any damned bears," John said to the belching man.

"Nah. Bears aren't common 'round here. Coyotes maybe. Didn't see any wolves on the way up here either. It'll be fine. Quit your worryin', criminal," the man responded.

They fed him a bit of unspecified meat and beans. He watched the belching man chow down on a pound of meat and six cans of beans, knocking back seven more bottles of beer before finally seeming content. John sat there dumbfounded about how much food this man could eat. The man was chubby but not big enough to need that much food in a sitting. John would be concerned if that man were a friend, but he could die for all he cared.

"Dammit, man! You drank all the beer!" Tom yelled at the man.

"Sorry, boss. I'm just so thirsty."

"Then go to the damn river and drink it dry for all I care. That was all we had for the trip back!"

That night, everyone slept except for John and the belching man. The man was two tents over, but John could hear him moaning and groaning as he tossed and turned the entire night. John lay on the bare ground, unable to sleep. He was surprised when the man just stopped. The silence was relieving, and John thought maybe he could finally sleep. Then the man started making a horrible gurgling sound like he was drowning. The belching man crawled out of his tent, blood pouring out of his mouth. He collapsed onto his stomach and rolled over onto his back. The light of the moon illuminated his face, showing that his eyeballs were bulging out of his head. John sat up, trying to wake Tom. As he did so, he watched the belching man stop moving once again.

An odd, fleshy, cracking noise started. John saw a hand burst from the man's stomach. The hand was thin, attached to a spindly arm, almost insect-like. Then another burst out. Both hands bent down and pushed their way out. The head was the most horrifying thing John had ever seen. The shock paralyzed him. He felt sweat drenching his body, and his limbs rattled with fear. The head had large, round black eyes and thin, needle-like teeth.

The little creature constantly made this odd clicking sound as it pulled itself out of the corpse of the belching man. When it was completely out of the belching man's corpse, it looked around. The creature saw John and grinned. Its mouthful of needle teeth made John jump, and he ran. His legs were still shackled, but he had forgotten in his panic, falling down into the grass. Blood poured out of his nose, but he got up and tried to keep going. He fell a few more times as the creature trailed behind him. He could hear the faint chittering of the creature clicking as it grew closer and closer. After an hour or so of running, John could see the outline of the town he came from.

John's knees and legs were exhausted from the trek and were close to buckling out from under him. He staggered to the inn where he had stayed and banged on the door. The innkeeper was still up at that late hour and answered.

"John! John Davis! I thought those Marshals took you away!"

"They did! Something… something killed one of them, and it came after me! I ran all the way here! Please! Please let me in!"

"Sure! Come in!" the innkeeper said as he closed the door. "What the hell happened?"

"A man, one of those Marshals, he died. Something burst out of his stomach and came after me."

"You're kidding?" The innkeeper said. He put his hand on John's head, "Well, I guess you're not running that fever any-more."

"No! It was no damned fever dream! I saw it!"

"Fine, fine. We will go to the sheriff in the morning."

"It can't wait until morning! That thing might be coming here!"

"Now, calm down, John. I'm sure it was a trick of light or.."

"No! It wasn't! That thing was real!"

"Okay, John. Sure. Well, your room is still open, and it's still paid for the night. Let's get you up there."

"That's nice of you, sir."

"I've only known you briefly, John, but Emilia and I agreed that you're no criminal. They must have mistaken you for someone else. We'll get this straightened out with the sheriff tomorrow. Maybe we can even get someone to break those chains off you."

The next morning, the innkeeper and John went to the Sheriff. John told them the story.

"Well damn, John. You must've eaten something weird out there!" the sheriff said as he laughed. "They say the natives would eat mushrooms that made them see things. Maybe you did, too?"

"No, I'm serious. If you go up there, they'll probably all be dead."

"Well, another funny thing is that I looked in all the bounties we've received from across all the western territories, but I don't have one for you. I think those Marshals were full of shit, if they're even Marshals. Who knows where they could've got those badges."

"We'll figure that out after you find their corpses, Sheriff."

"I'll take a couple of my deputies with me, and we'll go look. Meanwhile, I will have the doctor look at those wounds you got on you."

John went to the doctor's office one building over from the sheriff.

"Looks like you got into one hell of a fight," the doctor declared.

"Wasn't no fight, doc. I was runnin' for my life."

"I see. Well, just from glancing, I can tell that your nose is broken." The doctor said, while glancing around at John's face from various angles.

"Not the first time, and probably not the last."

"Well, we'll fix ya up and bandage up these cuts on your arms and legs. Nothing else looks broken to me."

Emilia came in with bandages. They locked eyes, but she didn't say a word to him. She made an awkward smile and didn't look at him again. He couldn't help but feel heartache from this. He left the doctor's office and went back to the inn.

"If you can spot me some grub, I'll pay ya back once the sheriff brings back my things."

"Don't worry about it, John. It's on the house. Emilia told me all about what happened. It's taken care of," the innkeeper offered.

Later that day, the Sheriff and his deputies came back, galloping fast into town, screaming for everyone to leave the town immediately.

"We have to evacuate the town! Now!" he screamed as he burst into the inn. The dozen patrons at the bar stopped talking at once and looked at him. His clothes and face were splattered with blood.

"What…" That was all John got out before he started hearing the God-awful chittering sound again.

"There's a hundred of them! They can fly! They ate those poor men to the bones! They're headed right towards us! I shot as many as I could! Dick got bit on the thigh, and James was slashed on his shoulder and arm! We have to get out of here!"

The chittering was now so loud that it blanketed all other noise. The sheriff slammed the door shut and dropped the wood bar to lock it. They all heard dozens of tiny feet touch down on the roof and saw even more outside on the ground. John watched out the window as a woman was knocked to the ground by one of the creatures, and her guts were ripped out.

There was even more screaming outside—some were children.

A voice rang out from throughout the tavern. "Sheriff! What in the hell is going on?"

"Sheriff! What are we going to do?"

"Sheriff! We have to help!"

Dozens of questions and suggestions were being flung at him.

The sheriff snapped, "Everyone shut the hell up!" and they did. "I'm hoping these doors will hold, but if they manage to get in, we will give them one hell of a fight," he said as he shoved a gun into John's chest.

Everyone in the tavern either drew out a pistol or searched for something to use as a weapon. During all this commotion, the Sheriff spoke to John.

"Found the piece you told me about. One of them, the fake Marshals, had it on them. All that I can figure is you killed one of their buddies, and they were out looking for revenge. I looked closely at one of their badges, which were completely fake. I feel stupid for failing to notice that before. I didn't have much time before these demon bugs from hell came flying over the trees toward us."

"Thanks, Sheriff," John replied. He felt some relief knowing the Sheriff believed him now.

"The rest of your stuff is on my horse if it's not dead," he said as he spat at the ground.

John had a sudden realization—was Emilia safe?

"Sheriff, I'm going to go check on the doctor. We could use him over here if someone gets hurt."

"That's a good point, but how will you get there without being ripped to pieces?"

"I'll just shoot my way through."

"You're kidding?"

"I'm a hell of a shot, Sheriff."

"I have a feeling you're going to do it, whether I say yay or nay."

"You're not wrong," John said, grinning. It was the first time he had smiled in a long time.

The sheriff lifted the bar on the front door and let John out, moving fast to close the door and lower the bar again. He told John to beat the hell out of the door to tell them it was him if he returned. He rushed outside. There were dozens of those little winged creatures on the roofs, scouring in all directions.

John shot one of the creatures that flew off the roof of the General Store across from the inn and shot another that was walking on the boardwalk. The Sheriff's horse was hitched near the inn, looking frightened out of its wits. The poor creature was pacing around circles in sheer terror. It was too far away for him to risk going after it. His gun was a six-shooter, so he had to wisely use these next four rounds. John ran diagonally across the dirt street to the doctor's office. The door wasn't locked, and the windows were still undamaged. He darted inside and locked the door behind him.

"Doctor Smith! Emilia! Are y'all okay?"

"I am!" Emilia answered. She was in the backroom where the doctor examined his patients.

John walked in and found her cowering in the back corner, shotgun cradled in her arms.

"Where's your husband?"

"He was outside when they came. One of them carried him off. I heard him screaming as they flew away. I don't know if he's dead or alive," she said as she cried. Her face was stained from the tears, her eyes bloodshot.

"Come with me! There's a bunch of us holed up at the inn until we can figure out what to do," John told her.

"No! I'm not leaving this spot! I'm safe here!"

"You're in a corner with no way out. If ten of those bastards busted through a window, do you really think you can shoot 'em all?"

"Yes! I most certainly can! I'm not a weak, pathetic woman! I can take care of myself!" she said as she jumped up, wiped her face with her sleeve, and stormed to the front. "Well, are you coming or not?"

"How much ammo you got?"

"Two pockets full. Now, come on!"

John was surprised by her tenacity, and he followed. She unlocked the door and shot two of them before she had taken more than a few steps out. They heard an explosion of glass coming from the inn. One of the creatures broke through the large front window, followed by several others. Screams erupted from inside.

Smoke started pouring from the broken window not long after. Someone knocked a lantern over, and the building quickly rose in flames. People were panicking. The door was still latched, but the fear caused people to ignore it as they tried to force it open. The creatures slashed and tore into the helpless people. The screams filled the now empty streets, louder than the chittering now.

"Oh shit! Let's get out of here!" John yelled. He grabbed Emilia by the arm and hauled her over to the Sheriff's horse. It was still alive and had stomped one of the creatures to death. Most of the creatures were preoccupied with what was happening at the inn and swarming to it like moths to a flame. One creature was zigzagging around the air, screeching and slashing at the horse. Emilia shot it down with ease. John pushed Emilia up onto the back of the horse, and then he climbed on.

Several hours later, the whole town would be reduced to ashes. John and Emilia were arrested by U.S. Marshals near Cheyenne, Wyoming.

"John Davis and Emilia Smith, you're both under arrest for arson and multiple counts of murder in the town of Irontown, Montana,"

As he was being arrested, John tried to argue his side, "Sir, we didn't do no such thing. It was an accident that caused that, not us!"

"Foolishness. We got a tip from Tom Prescott, a resident of that town, who said you had been planning on robbing the bank and killing as many people on your way out as you could. That the local sheriff didn't believe him. It's a shame we didn't get to you sooner."

"Bullshit! We would never do such a thing!" Emilia thrashed about, trying to overpower the man arresting her, but it was useless.

"I didn't do it! Neither did she! These are fucking absurd charges! You have no evidence!"

"We have the smoldering remains of Irontown as evidence. Now, come on. Your trial awaits."

HUNTER AND PREY

HE HAD TROUBLE REMEMBERING how he started on this journey. Was it when his father disappeared or when his brother, Caleb, died? None of that mattered anymore. He had been roaming the roads since he was sixteen years old, and he was now twenty-five. He was riding this bus thanks to a tip he found in the last town.

Keith dug his phone from his pocket and put on his earphones. He searched through podcasts he had downloaded and listened to one while he looked out the window, watching the endless rows of cacti and sand pass by. His mind drifted back to events from his past. He thought about all his friends back home and how much he missed them all. The pain of knowing he would never see them again sprouted again in his gut, but he tried to ignore it. Missing people would only slow him down.

In the several years that he had been traveling, Keith learned never to develop close relationships. They only distract you from your objective. The bus driver slammed on the brakes and started screaming.

"What the hell!?"

The driver tried to throw the bus into reverse, but his nerves caused him to fidget and miss gears, grinding chaotic calamity as he pumped the accelerator. Something slammed into the side of the bus, rocking it with enormous force. Everyone on the bus could hear the metallic grinding as the doors were pried apart.

A strange man stepped onto the bus. His clothes were weathered and old; a cowboy hat donned his head and a long—tailed coat that nearly dragged the floor trailing behind him. His boots scuffed as he walked. The man was wearing a piece of cloth around his face, like a Wild West bank robber in a movie. Deep, rattled breathing was coming under the cloth. The man looked around, searching the crowd. One of the old ladies started shouting at him, "What do you think you are? A damn cowboy? Get out of here, you!"

He grabbed her by the throat with reflexes quick as lightning. His abnormally long fingers wrapped around the old woman's wrinkled neck, and with one rapid twist, he tore her throat out. She slumped off the seat onto the floor, her eyes bulging out of her skull, blood shooting out of the hole where her throat had been. The other people on the bus began to panic. They all rushed to get off the bus, packing together at the rear exit in a mad rush. Another old lady fell as she tried to make her way to the exit, her walker knocked out from under her, and she was trampled on by the careless other riders who only focused on their own survival. The man shuffled to the back of the bus, his rattled breath becoming louder.

Keith noticed something as soon as the man stepped on the bus. He couldn't get up until he found the one weapon to kill it. It was stashed away in his carry-on bag. He had gone to great lengths to acquire the unique and extremely rare item. It was an ivory-handled dagger. Legend says that the ivory was carved from a dragon's fang. This dragon had ravaged eastern Europe for centuries, the last one in that entire section of the world.

Keith hurried, but was not fast enough to save those few people. He hated casualties—innocent people should never have to die. The strange man noticed Keith and noticed what he was doing. Inhuman growling and hissing came from under the cloth that wrapped his head. The strange man backed up, clawing at the air.

Keith began to recite a holy passage that he had memorized and used on several monsters before. Supposedly, the passage was written nine thousand years before in a dead language by a priest for a long-forgotten religion. The beast began maniacally growling and hissing now. Keith rushed the creature after he finished the passage. A few swift maneuvers later, he subdued the creature and stabbed it in the neck with the dagger. The strange man stopped. His skin turned charcoal gray and collapsed inward into its clothes. Keith inspected the clothing and found that only the ashes of the creature remained. In that ash, he found a large, carved ruby.

Keith went to the remaining people and consoled them for the next few hours after calling the local EMS.

"911. State your emergency."

"Yeah, our bus just wrecked. I think the driver had a heart attack. We are about ten miles north of Flagstaff on Route Eighty-nine. Two elderly people were hurt in the rollover. One of them is bleeding pretty bad."

"We'll get someone there as soon as possible."

Keith hung up and tried to tend to the people as much as possible. After regaining his composure, one of them asked Keith what the creature was.

"You really don't want to know," Keith said, cutting him off and walking away.

Some of the survivors were huddled in horror, crying over the trauma of what had happened, while others didn't make a sound. Keith walked along the road into the approaching darkness. Up ahead, he saw the lights of the EMS workers on the way, so he knew they would be safe. He could see a nearby town ahead, and he needed to hurry. Nighttime in the desert was different than anywhere else. Out here, there's nowhere to hide from the things that go bump in the night.

THE SHADOWS WILL GET YOU

"BUT WHY DO I HAVE TO go?" Lauren pleaded to her parents.

They were stern about it. There was no talking her way out of this one. Lauren stared out the window, watching the passing trees and houses zoom by as they drove along the back roads.

"You know why, Lauren. You've asked a thousand times, and we tell you the same answer," her mother answered, "It's because you've been in that room for months staring at that computer screen non-stop and drove yourself into this moody, depressed thing that we don't know as our Lauren. Your father and I agree that being in the country for the summer, away from high-speed Internet and cell phones, will cure that. Your uncle Victor and Aunt Charlotte happily accepted you to come down. You haven't seen your cousin Arthur since you were both toddlers."

Lauren could already feel the withdrawal. She had posted a dozen tweets and Facebook posts about how much she was going to hate it and how much she hated her parents.

"What am I supposed to do for fun?"

"Be a human and go outside. Enjoy what the Earth has to offer," her father responded. "Hey, look! The GPS says we are ten miles away now! You'll love it. Uncle Victor has some delicious food growing on that farm, and your Aunt Charlotte could beat Paula Deen. I guarantee it!"

"Yeah. Sure, Dad," Lauren rolled her eyes and turned the music up on her phone. Her earbuds played some melodramatic, over-emotional teen music as she watched more trees and fewer houses go by.

"We're here!" her father loudly announced so she could hear it over her music.

Lauren looked out the window and saw an enormous field filled with rows of wheat and corn. Their little house sat neatly in the middle, with their large yard and barn. The house was an old, white, two-story farmhouse with large windows in each room. Her uncle and aunt walked outside once the car doors slammed shut.

"Lauren! Oh, my Lord, you've grown so much! Look at you!" her aunt Charlotte said as she grabbed her by the face, kissing her multiple times.

"And Frank! You've turned gray!"

"Thanks, Charlotte. The mirror reminds me every morning."

"Don't feel bad. At least you have some." Victor said as he rubbed his balding scalp while he grinned.

"Alright, Lauren, Arthur would come to say hi, but he's busy with his nose in a book. His room is next to the guest room you'll stay in if you want to shake hands or whatever kids do to greet each other these days."

Lauren just stared at her in confusion as she went inside. "I'll show you in," her uncle Victor said as he finished a discussion with her father about the wheat.

"I got this farm from my father, ya know. He came here from Germany. Started off with a few seeds he got from the market that used to be down the road from here. All these damned superstores took that away. Farmer's markets are nice, but they don't compete, and they don't have the magic that those had," he rambled, "Anyway, when father got this, it was trees with nothing on it, but an old man owned it. He spoke a little German himself and told my father to beware the nightfall."

"You're telling me this why?"

"Well, at night, we lock all the animals up because we find them butchered in the yard in the morning if we don't. Kids in the area go missing, too. It only happens near this damned forest. It just does, and those are the rules. I will only warn you once, because that's all you'll probably get. Not even Arthur will. You won't see many cars, maybe passersby, but hardly any locals. All the stores stay brightly lit because they say it keeps it at bay, but don't ever venture out past your shadow. Understood?"

"Why the hell would my parents let me come to this loony bin? Seriously? Do you expect me to believe this or even care? I won't go anywhere anyhow because I don't know anyone, and I don't want to be here!"

"Now, there's no need to get snippy. Do as you're told," he said as he opened her room.

It was quite large. Almost twice as big as her room at home. The room had a dresser, a bed, a vanity mirror, and a large flat—screen TV hanging on the wall.

"Now, we have satellite TV, but there's no Internet or cell service for miles. We don't want it anyway. It's too distracting." he sat some of her bags on the bed. "Your Aunt will be up here in about an hour once dinner is done. That should give you time to unpack and get situated," he said, turned and started walking out the door, "But don't go outside after dark.. or the shadows will get you." he stared at her a few seconds to make sure she got the point and closed the door.

"Creepy hicks," she said under her breath while she dug through her bags.

When they called her down for dinner, she saw the table filled with food. It was close to a banquet. She had never seen anything so exquisite. Her uncle Victor noticed her wide eyes and laughed, "Honey, I think you've stunned the girl!"

"Sorry. I'm not used to something so… plentiful."

"This is how we eat here! Fill up at night, and you'll sleep like a bear!" Uncle Victor told.

"Right," she replied. She noticed Arthur for the first time.

He was a chubby kid with long hair and acne. He sat there, his nose buried deep in a book. Lauren knew they were only a few months apart, but couldn't help but notice how different they were.

She sat down and grabbed her spoon. Her Aunt smacked her hand.

"Not before Grace, young lady!" She shook her hand from the sting. "Sure. Yeah. Fine."

"May this food strengthen and nourish our bodies, and thank you for the beautiful woman who cooks for us every day. And also, may you guide Lauren down the right path of life toward you, Lord. In Jesus name, Amen!" her uncle Victor recited.

Lauren felt uncomfortable and didn't know how to react, so she waited for everyone else to eat before she started. The food was amazing, and she understood why her father remarked on Aunt Charlotte's cooking earlier. She agreed with him.

After dinner, she decided to speak with her cousin Arthur just so that awkwardness could be over with. She found him in his room, several books spread across his bed.

"Hey, Arthur."

He glanced up briefly and returned to his book. "Hey."

"Watcha reading?"

"Stuff."

"Oh. Well, sorry to bother."

She turned around, about to leave, and when he told her to wait, "The stuff Dad told you. It's true."

"Yeah, right. I don't believe…"

"No. Really. They got my friend, Billy."

"Really?"

"Yeah. They found him dead in his backyard. Cut up like a lawnmower ran over him. They found pieces of his skull all over the place. I regret ever finding that out."

"Is that what you're reading about?"

"I found some old books at the library. This goes back to even the Natives. They had legends about it, and they wouldn't even bother settling here. No one really did until artificial lights were first put in. Most people who did were either scared out or killed."

Her boredom intrigued her, so she grabbed his gamer chair and turned it so they could talk.

"So, what are they?"

"Don't know. The Natives just called them Vicious Shadows. We don't even call them a name here now, just shadows."

"Well, don't worry because I don't plan on going anywhere. I didn't want to come, but my parents insisted I get away. I will stay in my room for the next month until I can leave."

"There's a nice hiking trail behind the house if you get bored. I go up there sometimes. There's some neat Native American carvings up there."

That got her attention. She loved being outside. There was a great hiking trail a few miles from her house at a State Park that she liked.

"Let's go tomorrow. I haven't stretched my legs in a while," Lauren decided.

"Sure. We can do that."

The next day, she put on the closest thing she had to hiking boots, which she never considered packing, and grabbed a few necessities. The trail was a few miles long and passed a rocky outcrop with a small area under a ledge. That was where the Native carvings were.

"See, this is where the Natives would leave sacrifices for the shadows," Arthur told Lauren.

"That's f—," was all she got out before a sharp pain went through her skull.

She fell to the ground, the back of her head pumping blood all over her motionless body.

"Yes, cousin. They sure did sacrifice people here. I'm sorry, but they're hungry. It's either you or us," Arthur spoke out loud while holding the bloody ball-peen hammer.

She woke up lying in a pool of her own blood. It still hurt, and the blood had coagulated in her hair into knots. She still pulled back some fresh, but it was mostly dry now. She was delirious, and her head throbbed endlessly.

"Where... what?" she stammered. "Arthur! Arthur!" She looked around. She saw nothing, nothing but shadows.

LISTEN CLOSE

"GREETINGS, OUR DEAR and beloved listeners! Tonight is the season premiere of the Horrifying Tales podcast!" the announcer proclaimed through my earbuds.

I remember the rain was coming down hard that night, and my upstairs bedroom amplified those sounds quite well. I had my laptop placed across my thighs while I sat on my bed, browsing through Facebook and Twitter as I usually did when I was bored. On Facebook, there were reports coming in of downed power lines from the torrential downpour.

Outside, it was pitch black, but the power was still on somehow. I like the sound of rain; it helps me relax. Around that time, I had just been dumped by my longtime girlfriend. We had been dating for about two years, which was what my nineteen—year-old self would classify as long-term. By that point, she was with some guy who thought he would be the next Kurt Cobain. I had decided to medicate myself with a little pot, and it always enhances that podcast.

"Now, here is a story by a new writer to the podcast. I have a special message for those of you out there who are listening to this alone, so you might want to—Listen Close!"

After getting a little blazed, I decided to look up my ex's recently posted pictures to see what she and her new boyfriend were up to. They looked happy, or at least in the pictures they did. There were selfies of them in the car and in restaurants, and worst of all, lying on her bed together. It had been a few months since the breakup, but I still hadn't completely healed. When the announcer stated I should listen closely, that got my attention.

"Cole Tanner sat on his bed, bored and paying no attention to the world around him, as he tended to do," the narrator started.

"Cole Tanner? What the hell? That's my name!"

"His mom and stepdad were out grocery shopping, so he was lazing around while they were gone."

I laughed a little at this. Even I could admit that I was a lazy kid.

"He started feeling hungry after smoking the few joints he had left, so he started to head toward the stairs that lead down into the kitchen so he could search for something quick to eat."

I froze because that's exactly what I was doing. At first, I thought it was the pot, but the story continued.

"He froze, feeling the hair rise on the back of his neck like someone was breathing on him."

Chills ran down my spine. That's exactly what I was feeling. I was too afraid to look, too afraid to spin around. What if someone was there? What would I do? I overcame the fear after a few seconds and turned my head very slowly, carefully, checking. Nothing was there.

"And he saw nothing. That eerie feeling still resonated in his mind as he returned down the stairs. He looked around, careful to check that nothing was about to jump around the corner." I actually didn't think of that, but it sounded like a good idea.

The story somehow narrated everything I was doing, down to the exact second. I thought about turning it off, but I was enjoying it so far and wanted to see how this went.

"Cole reached into the fridge, hunting for leftovers that he could warm in the microwave. He had no such luck. That was when he heard a loud click as the power shut off in the house. In almost an instant, the only sound was the rain."

"Bang! Bang! Bang! Something was bashing on the window above the kitchen sink. Cole could see nothing until a powerful lightning flash illuminated the darkness. Staring at him was the disfigured face of a bearded man wearing a rain slicker."

Cole backed up as the podcast was playing heart-pounding music.

"Cole bolted up the stairs, trying not to fall on his hasty retreat back to his bedroom. Halfway up, he heard the explosion of glass shattering. The crazed man had busted in the kitchen side door, desperately trying to grab the door handle."

To say that I was panicking by this point would be an understatement. I stumbled a few times up the stairs. I looked back and saw only darkness. Then the lightning flashed again, and I saw that he was even closer, just two steps below me. The cord for the ladder to the attic was not far from the top of the stairs. As fast as I could scramble, I jerked that ladder down and scurried up.

"Desperately, Cole tried to close the ladder, but the maniac was too quick for him. He leaped and grabbed the bottom rung, almost yanking Cole down with it. He exclaimed and backed into the corner of the attic, bumping into something. He couldn't see it from the darkness, but turned the flashlight on from his phone. What he forgot about was the gun case that his mother put up there after his father was killed in the line of duty. It was his father's gun."

I totally forgot about that. It was true. The case did have Dad's gun in it. I was mystified, but also relieved that it was there. I knew the combination and Dad's birth date and opened the lock. Inside, I found a loaded magazine. Why it was loaded, I don't know; maybe Mom had kept it for emergencies, but why keep it in the attic? Dad had taken me shooting once or twice, and my uncle Don had been taking me every other weekend since Dad's passing. Don was also an officer and said it was important to know how to shoot. He wasn't wrong about that.

I loaded that pistol, cocked it, and emptied three rounds into the intruder's chest as he made his way across the attic floor.

He was probably five feet or so from me by that time. He would've gotten me if I had been just a few seconds longer. I stood up, surveyed his body, and after a minute or so, decided that it was time to get out of that room and call 911.

"Cole was stepping over the lifeless body of the maniac when a hand grasped his ankle. Cole looked down and saw the maniac staring at him, blood pouring from his mouth. The maniac gurgled something, then his head hit the floor with a thud, and his hand loosened its grip on Cole's ankle long enough for him to run."

I ran down that ladder and the stairs faster than I ever had in my life. I didn't call 911 until I had made it outside and was sure that I was safe. I had decided to hide in the garage behind some boxes until the police arrived. They were there within thirty minutes, even with the ongoing storm. Luckily, the fire department had already cleared all the trees off the road. With them came my mom and stepdad, John. The situation freaked him out, and he did his best to make us all feel safe. Mom was concerned with consoling me, asking at least a hundred times if I was okay. It was annoying at the time, but now I'm glad I've always had her.

I never told anyone about the podcast or that story. About a year later, I tried to find it so I could listen to it again, but it was not on the list of episodes. The episode listed for that week was an entirely different episode.

I wanted to save this for last because I think it's the best part. At the end, the narrator says the author's name.

"Hopefully, you… listened close. I want to reiterate that this was from a new author. We want to thank Marshall Tanner for contributing to the show and hope to hear more from him soon."

Marshall Tanner was my father's name.

REAP

WORDS CANNOT DESCRIBE the fear that I felt that night. I knew it was cold outside, so I threw my robe over my thin night-gown and grabbed the candle sitting on a table next to the door. The being was close to me, but I wouldn't let it get me. I could hear it slinging the scythe it carried, sometimes feeling the wind off the blade.

My husband and I were warming by the hearth fire earlier that night. He was sharpening his knife on a wood block while I knitted some clothing with the approaching snow. A knocking came at the front door. Curious, I answered, and a tall man stood, bundled head to toe in black.

"It's cold. Please let me in," his voice was deep, almost guttural, and eerie as could be. He stood there shivering, his arms wrapped across his chest tightly. It wasn't quite that cold, but enough to be uncomfortable. My husband looked him over and said to let him in.

We gave him some leftover stew, which he ate like he had not eaten in a month. His face was scarred and covered in a thick gray beard.

"Thank ye both. T'was kind of ye," he told us.

"Tis not a problem, stranger. Christ would do the same," my husband said to him.

He nodded his head. "Indeed, he would."

We didn't have a lot of money, but we made do. My husband was a blacksmith and strong as an ox. He and some of the men from town built our home themselves. We had three bedrooms, which was large compared to the hovels most people in our village lived in. We had the other two bedrooms turned into guest rooms and occasionally rented them out.

Childbearing wasn't as easy as we thought, and as I was approaching thirty years old, there was little hope of pregnancy. My husband said he was fine with it and that he loved me just the same.

My husband took the strange man to his room and bid him goodnight. We went upstairs and to bed ourselves. We heard nothing from the man before falling asleep, not even a snore. At some point in the night, we were awakened by an enormous thump that shook the house.

"Don't get up, dear. Stay in bed. I'll investigate," my husband said as he put on his leathers and sword.

About a minute later, I heard the sounds of a commotion, the sound of something slashing, then a scream and a thud. The silence was after that. I was terrified. I disobeyed my husband and went downstairs. There, I found him dead. His throat had been slashed clean to the spine.

Then, in a distant corner of the room, I saw it. That was not a man any longer, but some demon. There was no face, just bright orange eyes that flickered like flames! In its hand was a scythe. I ran to the door, threw on my robe, and grabbed a lit candle, dashing out the door into the darkness of the night.

The demon was standing over me now, its flaming eyes staring into me.

"What say you, woman? What say you for your sins and your husbands?"

"I say nothing."

That was when I began my transformation. Being a werewolf came in handy sometimes. I don't know if demons can show fear, but that one sure seemed frightened. It took off toward the woods. I was on it in moments. I ripped apart the robes only to find a decaying human body underneath, most likely the person it had possessed.

I howled at the moon in victory, and I heard a howl back in the distance. In our house, I found my husband had regained consciousness, his throat nearly healed.

"Did you take care of it?"

"Yes, husband. There will be more."

"I know, wife, but there is one less demon roaming around in human flesh."

"We may have to fight them off for the rest of our lives."

"And I would be happy to do, with you by my side."

There are plus sides to being a werewolf. For one, you are immortal. That particular story was three hundred years ago. We now reside in the countryside of Scotland. We have a small farm and raise sheep, making our money off their wool and meat. We live a peaceful life, but on occasion, another one of those damned creatures comes for us. What they don't know is that we are always ready.

CUT ITS HEAD OFF

ONE THING YOU MUST REMEMBER about when I was born is that people were very paranoid. Everything was a bad omen, and everything that went bad was because of the devil and his evil little minions. Of course, people capitalized on this fear. Dozens of fake, deceitful people made a lot of money from declaring evil was there and getting rid of it, and most of them got away without ever being caught.

I was one of them for a while and made a lot of money. Sometimes, even town governments would hire us to cleanse them of evil spirits. On occasion, I would hire someone to help me. We would drill holes in the walls of houses and make an amplification device to make it seem like evil spirits were talking to them or project sounds like the famous chain-rattling sound people often claimed to hear. It was all fun and games until the year 1892, when I was summoned to a village in southern England called Donnerton.

I was at my home in London at the time, having just returned from a long trip to Germany, when a messenger came to my door. The young man handed me a message addressed to the Village Government of Donnerton. It wasn't the first time I had been summoned by a mayor or town council. The message said that in the last week, seven people had been attacked by vampires, but none of their efforts seemed to have an effect on the problem. I immediately sensed something off about this one, unlike other requests I had received over the years. Vampirism was something I had been requested for often, and normally, it was just an outbreak of typhoid or some other disease that caused vampiric symptoms.

Upon arrival, I was greeted by the minuscule town council.

The mayor hugged me and kissed me on both cheeks.

"Mr. Benjamin Elwin! Hunter extraordinaire! Thank God for you! Thank God you're here!"

I noticed the mayor looked visibly exhausted. Most likely hadn't slept a night in days, possibly that whole week that he mentioned in his letter.

"Good day, Mayor Darby. I will do as much as God will allow me. I pray he gives me the power to dispatch these beasts."

See, you had to emphasize the whole religious aspect, or they wouldn't take you seriously.

"I certainly hope you can resolve this matter! Now, I will have this young man here escort you to the inn we have arranged for you. I hope you can begin tonight?"

"I most certainly can start tonight." I smiled. Smiling is key, too; it shows confidence. "I have but two requests, Mayor."

"Most certainly! What would those be?"

"One, a bottle of your best wine. Two, a nice dinner to go with the wine."

He thought this was funny. Humor always helped, "Yes! Neither of those is out of the question!"

I had acquired a good sum of money in my business, and so I tried to dress the part. Regarding any form of business, showing off your wealth is key. I removed my top hat, jacket, and vest in my room, rolled up my sleeves, and unpacked my bags. There was a lot of popular lore about vampires that one had to ensure you were prepared to address when questioned. I brought all the necessities: a wooden stake, a necklace of garlic, a trusty silver crucifix and holy water, and a small hatchet to remove the head. I kept them in a roll-out bag with slots for each item, which I thought suggested that I was more professional than my competitors.

I asked for a second-floor room to trot around peacefully without disturbing the guests on the first floor. This wasn't my first experience with a supposed outbreak of vampirism. After thinking, I supposed I would have to bring in outside help to be the vampire. It was late at night when I started writing my letter. That was when I heard a knocking at my window.

At first, I just assumed it was a nearby tree, but human curiosity took the best of me, and I had to look. It wasn't a tree. I saw a gray-skinned man at my window with deep crimson eyes. He was grimacing until he noticed that I saw him. He grinned, revealing a mouth full of pointed, carnivorous fangs. It knocked again, this time slower and harder, as if impatiently.

After saving myself from a fall out of my chair, I scrambled on my hands and knees across the floor for my gear. I grabbed the crucifix and the holy water from my bag and rushed near the window as close as my anxiety-rattled brain would allow me. I showed it to the crucifix and tossed holy water onto the window.

The thing laughed at me. It was a deep, raspy laugh, making my body run cold.

I heard it say through the window, "God will not save you, boy. Your legends are false, just like your God." It laughed some more. "Now, let me in!"

There was something that the legends left out that I wished I had known prior; if you look them in the eyes long enough, you are wrapped in a haze of hypnosis. Out of my mind and not realizing what I was doing, I walked over to the window and unlatched it, letting the thing in.

"Yes. Good boy. Yes!"

It stepped inside. Its clothes were ragged and rotted, and the thing absolutely reeked of the scents of death.

"Now, lie down, boy. I'm hungry."

Somehow, I don't know if it was God or just adrenaline, but for a moment, I snapped out of my hypnosis and went for the stake lying at the end of the bed. In a swift maneuver, I swung it at the thing. The stake gouged in the side of its neck. The beast hissed and growled, contorting in the air like it had been horrifically burned.

"You bastard! I will kill you for this!" it screamed, while still twisting and hissing.

There was something else from the lore that I remembered; you must remove their head. I went for the hatchet and swung with everything I had. The ax planted in the thing's skull, and it dropped with a thud. It took a few minutes to get the head off, but I cut its head off. According to the lore, you also had to burn the remains to remove the evil completely. I made haste and shoved the remains out of the window, which landed in the garden. The innkeeper was sleeping when I found him, so I woke him and asked for kindling.

"Why on earth would you need that in the summer? At this hour even?"

"I killed a vampire, John. I need to burn the remains."

Shocked, he got out of bed and obliged. He took me to the woodshed, and we made an impromptu pyre. He couldn't believe the creature that was lying on the ground in pieces.

"That looks like it used to be Leonard Hathaway, but he died a month ago!"

"Perhaps not, John."

We stood by and watched it burn. The oddest part was that the flames were not your typical red and orange, but black and a deep blue, nor was there smoke. The flames burned until dawn. It took hours before I could sleep, and that was only a mere nap. After consuming copious amounts of tea, I went into town to search for clues. I wouldn't have said that I was much of an investigator at the time, and I had never actually investigated with honest purposes before. It was a mild Sunday afternoon in mid-July, and the church was in full swing, so I went there.

"Come! Sit, Mr. Elwin! Come join us!" he said as I went inside, "This is the young man here to assist us with our… problem." The old, gray-haired man introduced me.

"Hello," I said, waving awkwardly. If only they knew what I had endured the night before. I never have much time for conversation because of lack of sleep.

"Anyway, back to the topic. We must not forget that God is always watching over us and will protect us in our time of need." As he paced back and forth onstage, the preacher said, "This is one of those dire times in which our faith in God should not be shifted because if we give in, even just a little, we may lose everything. Remember Job, remember what he went through. Let not the Devil shake your foundation…" And so on and so forth.

After an hour, I started asking church people to come to the inn. The innkeeper was nice enough to let me use his office. One old lady said Satan himself was coming to claim the Earth for his kingdom, and we were all doomed. She didn't divulge much more than that paranoid delusion. Another man came in and stated, a few days before it all began, that the local salt mine owner was seen bringing home a very large shipment in the middle of the night. Rumor had it that they had an almost dangerous fascination with science. People back then were wary of science because many believed it tampered with God's creations and power and that one should not do such things.

After listening to a few more people inform me that Satan was coming, I made my way to the manor, which was located a few miles outside of the village. The manor was in a field with grazing cattle, watching me as I rode on horseback. Attached to the side of the manor was a high tower with a veranda on top for a high view of the surrounding countryside. I approached the door when the servant stopped me. He was an older, white—haired man with a thick mustache to match.

"Good day, sir. How may I be of service today?"

"Good day to you, too, sir. I am Benjamin Elwin. As of late, I was hired to investigate some odd goings-on in this village, and part of my investigation has led me here. May I speak with the lord of this manor?"

"He is out of town for a while. His mother back in Leicester is ill, and he has returned home to be with her."

"I see. Very well. I shall return later. How much longer will he be gone?"

"That, I do not know, sir. Mr. Burke will be back when he is able to. Shall I message you when he does?"

"No need. I'm not sure how long I'll be. Thank you anyway. Good day."

I turned around and went back to my room at the inn. A dead-end was not what I needed, and nightfall was coming soon. The mayor agreed to have two men stay with me that night. We decided we would wander the village and watch for anything out of the ordinary. The two men he hired were former military, and he said they were good with a musket, but I wasn't sure if that would help much. I let them arm themselves with their best rifle.

It was about an hour after sunset when we saw the first one.

It was banging on the window of an elderly widow. We could hear her inside screaming for God to save her. Clarence shot the thing in the head, incapacitating it. It still shrieked and moaned, but I removed the head with my hatchet. We created a pyre before sundown and tossed the remains into it. The second we spotted at the home of a family of six, and we did the same with that one. We spotted the third and last one toward the end of the night. It was following us, hiding in the shadows. Jonathan spotted it and took it down in one shot. It lunged at him, but he jabbed it with his bayonet, shooting it in the head seconds later. That one went on the pyre as well. The night's flames were strong and just as black and blue as the first.

What was going on was now undeniable. The mayor and I decided we had to hold a town meeting before anyone else died.

He sat down and made this speech, but I decided I would tell them what I knew—vampires were assaulting their town.

"People! Calm down! We are here to have an informative meeting and to fill you all in on what we know." The mayor began. "So, as far as we know, it started a few nights ago when the corpse of Jude Garner was found by his wife the following morning. Alan Chambers was the first to see one of those unholy beasts and reported it to me when he did. Since then, with the assistance of Mr. Elwin, we have killed seven of those demons, each night increasing in number. We are here to inform you on how to fight them, how to prepare yourselves, and assistance with leaving if you choose to do so."

There was a silence that hung over that place that was filled with anxiety. I walked up to him and stood beside him at the preacher's podium.

"Keep in mind that we will win this. God will not allow evil to triumph, and neither will I."

"Thank you, Mr. Elwin." While wiping sweat from his brow with his white handkerchief, the mayor said, "Now, who wants to leave? I will give you one hour to discuss this with your loved ones."

During that hour's discussion, the mayor informed me that the town currently had about two-hundred-ninety-three people, nearly all the men working in the salt mine. They were very religious people who clung tightly to the local Catholic church. He feared a considerable number of them would choose to leave, resulting in the town's downfall. His fears were confirmed later.

When we returned to the front area of the church, the mayor stood before the crowd and raised his hands to quiet everyone.

"Now, it is still early in the day, so please, everyone, sit down, except for all those who want to leave."

Understandably, almost the entire crowd stood. I counted twelve still sitting. The mayor was audibly upset, in which I could not blame him. "Those who want to leave, no one can stop you, but remember, this is also where your jobs and livelihoods are. This is your home you're abandoning! You worked hard here, and some of you grew up here. Surely more of you will stay and fight?"

"There are jobs elsewhere, Mayor." One man proclaimed. "God will follow us no matter where we go." A woman said. "We don't want to die at the hands of Satan!" a man shouted. Many voices stated they agreed.

"But people, this is where your homes are…" Before the mayor could finish, people started standing up and walking out the doors.

"This is the end of Donnerton, Mr. Elwin. We have lost." The mayor proclaimed, glum, as a mother who had lost her children. I felt terrible for him, but didn't know how to console him.

It was noon by then, and by the end of the day, most of those families had left town in search of better things elsewhere. Donnerton was a husk of what it was before. The thriving little village was now almost vacant. I sat with the mayor and watched as he drank his way to the bottom of a bottle of Scotch. I tried to keep the topics on anything but the vampires.

After I left, I went straight to my room at the inn. The innkeeper had decided to stay. I thought about getting a drink at the pub on the first floor, but decided I should get prepared instead. People or not, these things were coming. I considered leaving them, but I committed to cleansing this town. The Mayor hired me, and he honestly wanted to fight to save his beloved village. Only a few others and I had remained to take on the undead. The men I had used as my assistants had decided to leave town. I tried to gather others, but none were willing. They had boarded up their windows and put various religious articles around their doors to drive them away. I tried telling them it wouldn't work, but they wouldn't hear me.

I was walking the streets that night when I turned a corner on the main road in town. Before me stood what could have been one hundred of them, if not more. They all stood still—a primal hunger visible on their gray faces.

A voice called out, "Children! We have an empty town! What fun is this?"

From the crowd walked a man wearing old battle armor.

The armor was pristine and well-shined, but his face was as gray as the rest. I remember there being a golden, fire-breathing dragon's head adorning on the breastplate.

"Mr. Elwin. I am well informed of your exploits. You almost found me, you know. You were at the right place; you didn't try hard enough. Thankfully, the servant was clever enough to shoo you away," He laughed, "The owner of this mine brought me here. He is, or was, a collector of rare antiquities. Word reached him that someone was selling an old vampire corpse all the way in Kyiv.

"When I arrived, he ran experiments on me, doing this and that, until he came across an old book on how to raise the dead. Turns out, it even works on vampires." He was laughing very heartily. "Little did he know that I would turn on him. I tore his throat out with ease. Then I went to the local cemetery and started raising people with his book, then turning them into one of us. Now, I have an army. Can you chop all of our heads off, Mr. Elwin?"

I turned and ran. I made the reasonable decision that I was nowhere near prepared to take on fifty-odd vampires single handedly. He was laughing and mocking me as I ran. My brain raced to find a solution when something dawned on me. This mine should have a large supply of dynamite stored somewhere.

The mine was at the back of the town, up the hill a way, but they stored all their supplies near the inn. I knew this from my brief explorations around town the last few days. Everything that I needed was in that building. In haste, I made a torch out of a fallen tree branch and a rag that I soaked in oil. They were gathering around me.

"What do you plan on doing with that? Set us all on fire?" the armored one said.

"No," I said as I struck a match, "This."

I threw the torch on the stacks of crates marked as containing dynamite and ran like hell. I made it about two hundred feet before the explosion knocked me to the ground, rendering me unconscious.

When I woke up, I was in a hospital bed with burns on my face and arms. This is the story they told me: the explosion blew me into a creek, and thankfully not headfirst, so I survived severe burns that way, but my exposed parts were still burned from the sheer heat. The explosion leveled five surrounding houses and caused a fire to ravage the other houses in the village.

The fire brigade had all abandoned the town earlier that day, so there was no one to quell the flames. Most of the remaining citizens fled when the explosions rocked the earth, and only two people died. The odd thing, the doctor told me, was that the rescuers had found these piles of ashes with bones in random places across the town and a terribly scorched set of armor on a street.

Now you're wondering how I'm telling you this story well over a hundred years later. As you see, after this little venture, I was turned on another expedition in northeast France, which was later destroyed during the First World War. I found a doctor, a not very sane one at that, who claimed to know all these extraordinary things, like curing vampirism. Well, it didn't cure me, but it did put the symptoms at bay. My only issues are daylight and this horrifically pale skin. I still consider myself human, as I don't crave blood or the taste of human flesh.

Anyway, this is my story, and this is also my request. I aim to rid the world of all vampires, and I need your help.

Do you think you have the balls to kill a vampire?

THE VENGEFUL CHRISTMAS GHOST

THE HOWLING WINDS WERE roaring
As the sound of peace filled the room
I listened to my dog snoring
And the only thoughts on my mind were doom

First came the rapping at the front door
"Who is it?" I called
Not a sound came anymore
The reading of my book had stalled

I opened the door to investigate
Who would bother me
During such an icy, snowy day
There was not a soul to see

"Where are you? What do you want?"
I called into the blowing, frozen air
But the quiet did taunt
Where could they go on such a frigid dare?

Inside, I found such a fright
My heart nearly stopped
My eyes could not believe such a sight
As my wordless jaw dropped
Stacked on the table, high in a pile
Stood all four chairs

Perfectly assembled high
While I was unaware
I thought about leaving
My hand went for the door
But I knew that scheming
It would leave me trapped outdoors

I prayed the Lord's Prayer
Then, he begged for His protection
Against this evil despair
And my own reflection

"You killed me," a voice called out
I stopped, nearly fainting
The thoughts that my mind had shut out
By the justification of his slaying

"Whom is this accusing?"
"My name is of no importance
Is my death so inducing?
That you flail in your arrogant portance?"

"You killed me out of spite
Your heart is hard as stone
And your mind is full of ice
Just as you will die on this fateful night."

Through the snow, I dashed
"Run as far as your legs will go."
The muzzle flashed
As I fired my pistol at the empty snow
A hollow laugh echoed through the waning light
The cold growing into my soul
I had to survive; I had to fight
Through this frigid, icy stroll

As the light began to fade
I took one last look behind
To see what fate I had made
The old man standing in the cabin light

The wound on his face was wide and bloody
From the ax, I used to chop
While he napped in the study
To the floor, his body dropped

There had been stories and rumors
Of the gold he stashed away
Under the kitchen floorboards
 And inside the mattress of hay

Oh, the stories of gold were true
Bars, jewelry, and coins
With the plunder, I paid a crew
That cabin was built from purloin

I hid the rest far into the hills
I thought if I could make it there
I could pay for any way that I will
To get as far from this cabin of despair
The snow seemed to deepen with every step
Soon, I was buried to the waist
I feared I was inching closer to death's doorstep
But I had to continue without haste

"Trudge through the snowy mire,
As far as your body may take you,
But you will never see another flicker of fire,
Except until your hellish debut."

I reached the spot in another hour
To find it had been looted
A thief had been so coward!
To rob me in such a time ill-suited

The old man laughed with glee
"There is nothing better,
But to see you on your knees,
When you really have paid your debtor!"

"Run! Run now, evildoer,
Run to the end of your life,

Run to your eternal immure,
Run to the end of your strife!"

The darkness of night was blinding
Only the blinding void was in sight
The bitter cold never biting
There seemed to be little time
Then I was falling, tumbling down
The rocks became my cushion
My jaw cracked, and a broken crown
My mortality began to breakdown

I couldn't move!
I couldn't budge!
I was trying to prove
That I could even nudge

The heat of my blood ran
Down my face and eyes
Bone split open like a grin
I had no more time

"'Tis justice, I would say,
To see you in such a place,
To see you in such a way,
In no better way could I state,
That you are getting your reward,
Killing me in your utter greed,
Split open like a gourd,
This is most deserving, indeed!

'Tis the best Christmas I could imagine,
The only wish my restless soul wanted,
To see your end in this fashion,
You will soon meet your end of days!
Now I bid you farewell,
As the angels call me home,
And you will burn in hell,
Good luck in your volcanic catacomb!"

I watched the wind blow,

The snow blanketed my body,
The only thing left to feel was cold,
As the heat began burning my soles.

ABOUT THE AUTHOR

Brandon Wills was born and raised in West Virginia. He has been reading, writing, and telling stories since he was old enough to do so. He writes for Paranormality Magazine, is a member of the Horror Writers Association, the WV Writers, Inc., and is part of the Wild & Weird Radio podcast. He still lives in West Virginia with his wife, Emily, and three children, Paisley, Brody, and Bryce, along with their plethora of cats, dogs, and chickens.